"You're Not Going To Get Undressed Here, Are You?"

"No." In fact, Rick wasn't thinking about undressing himself, but her. What the hell was going on here? This was a business relationship. She was Alessandra Lawrence, chairman of the board. The one who fired him.

So why did he want to rip off her suit and take her right on the bed?

Because she was a beautiful woman. He'd always suspected as much, of course. But with her conservative suits and reserved manner, he never saw her as anything more than a wolf in sheep's clothing. He had her pegged as an uptight prude.

But there was something about her now that gave him pause. She had a quality, a way about her. There was a spark there. A connection. But whatever it was, it needed to be ignored. She was off-limits. Forever and always.

This whole thing was make-believe. And he needed to keep it that way.

Dear Reader,

It's November and perhaps the weather is turning a bit cooler where you are…so why not heat things up with six wonderful Silhouette Desire novels? *New York Times* bestselling author Diana Palmer is back this month with a LONG, TALL TEXANS story not to be missed. You've loved Blake Kemp and his ever-faithful assistant, Violet, in other books…. Now you finally get their love story, in *Boss Man*.

Heat continues to generate in DYNASTIES: THE ASHTONS with Laura Wright's contribution, *Savor the Seduction*. Grant and Anna shared a night of passion some months ago…now he's wondering if they have a shot at a repeat performance. And the temperature continues to rise as Sara Orwig delivers her share of surprises, in *Highly Compromised Position,* the latest installment in the TEXAS CATTLEMAN'S CLUB: THE SECRET DIARY series. (Hint, someone in Royal, Texas, is pregnant!)

Brenda Jackson gets things simmering in *The Chase Is On,* another fabulous Westmoreland story with a strong emphasis on food…tasty! And Bronwyn Jameson is back with the conclusion of her PRINCES OF THE OUTBACK series. Who wouldn't want to share body heat with *The Ruthless Groom?* Last but not least, get all hot and bothered in the boardroom with Margaret Allison's business-becomes-pleasure holiday story, *Mistletoe Maneuvers*.

Here's hoping you find plenty of ways to keep yourself warm. Enjoy all we have to offer at Silhouette Desire.

Best,

Melissa Jeglinski

Melissa Jeglinski
Senior Editor
Silhouette Books

Please address questions and book requests to:
Silhouette Reader Service
U.S.: 3010 Walden Ave., P.O. Box 1325, Buffalo, NY 14269
Canadian: P.O. Box 609, Fort Erie, Ont. L2A 5X3

MISTLETOE MANEUVERS

MARGARET ALLISON

Published by Silhouette Books

America's Publisher of Contemporary Romance

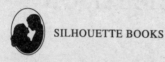 SILHOUETTE BOOKS

ISBN 0-373-76692-0

MISTLETOE MANEUVERS

Copyright © 2005 by Cheryl Guttridge Klam

This edition published by arrangement with Harlequin Books S.A.

Visit Silhouette Books at www.eHarlequin.com

Printed in U.S.A.

MARGARET ALLISON

was raised in the suburbs of Detroit, Michigan, and received a B.A. in political science from the University of Michigan. A former marketing executive, she has also worked as a model and actress. The author of several novels, Margaret currently divides her time between her computer, the washing machine and the grocery store. She loves to hear from readers. Please write to her c/o Silhouette Books, 233 Broadway, Suite 1001, New York, NY 10279.

For my sister, Jenny, with love.

One

It was nearly midnight, two weeks before Christmas, and for the first time in months they were alone. As if anticipating what was to come, Rick grinned, silently daring her. Tall and ruggedly handsome, with thick black hair and piercing blue eyes, Rick Parker was the type of man who was accustomed to getting what he wanted. A modern-day pirate, he traveled the world collecting beat-up hotels, jewels in the rough, turning them into luxurious resorts.

It was now or never. Lessa took a breath of courage, determined to say the three words she had wanted to say for years. She was so close she could smell his expensive aftershave, so close she could smell the minty freshness of his breath.

"You're fired, Rick."

The muscles in his jaw tightened and his eyes darkened as the impact of her words sank in. "I'm not going to let you take this company away from me," he said.

A flicker of apprehension coursed through her. After all, this was the man who had orchestrated a corporate mutiny, betraying his own mentor. Since then his domineering style of management had turned Lawrence Enterprises into a behemoth of a company, earning its fearless leader his pirate nickname along the way. What, she couldn't help but wonder, would he do to her?

But if he thought a threat would help save his job, he was wrong. She had promised her father on his deathbed that she would get revenge on the man who had stolen his company. That she would one day fire Rick Parker.

Since she had returned to the business six months ago, Rick had only added to her determination. He had done his best to thwart her path, treating her more like an annoying schoolgirl than an accomplished businesswoman. He fought her on every aspect of her agenda, from the color of the new logo to the direction of the company. It was as if he still considered her the same girl who had suffered a crush on him so fierce that a mere glance in her direction could cause her heart to soar. He should've realized he had lost his power over her long ago. He couldn't make her walk the plank any more than he could swindle her out of the company. "There's nothing you can do," she said. "I am chairman of the board."

"A situation that has everything to do with stock and nothing to do with expertise."

"My father had always intended for me to run this company. I've worked long and hard for this moment, Rick. I own a majority and I'm qualified. I've paid my dues."

"Your father may have started this company but I am the one who made it what it is. This company needs me."

"No, Mr. Parker. This company does not need you. Neither do I."

He leaned backward, crossing his arms. "The board is in agreement?"

In fact, she had had to struggle for the board's approval to fire Rick. Ultimately, they had had no choice but to agree with her. After all, as Rick had just said, she owned two thirds of the stock. "Yes," she said.

There was no mistaking the glimmer of anger in his eyes. He stood up and turned his back on her as he walked to the window. From their vantage point on the top floor of a New York City high-rise, he had a bird's-eye view of the twinkling city, lit up for the impending holiday.

"I don't want to hurt you, Alessandra," he said, referring to her by her full name, which was seldom used.

"Hurt me?" If she wasn't mistaken, she was the one who had fired him.

"I guarantee you, if you go through with this, you'll regret it." He turned around to face her.

"I don't think so," she said. Who did he think he was anyway? She stood up and straightened her suit jacket. "I've read your contract. You have a noncompete clause. Due to your work and contributions to this company, I will grant you some of the dignity you did not extend to my father. You have until the end of the day tomorrow to clear out your office."

"So this is your revenge, is it?" he asked. "You should know I didn't have anything to do with the way your father was fired."

"You may not have pulled the trigger but you were the one who loaded the gun." Bravo. That was a line she had worked on, one she never actually thought she would say. She gave him a quick, curt nod. "Goodbye, Rick."

She could almost feel his eyes watching her as she walked out of his office. She shut the door behind her and let out a sigh of relief as she leaned up against it. She had done it. She had fired Rick Parker and lived to talk about it. She had expected a bloody uprising, a long and drawn-out war. But in one anticlimactic moment, it was over. All of her years of study and work had paid off. Rick Parker would not be a part of her life or her father's company anymore.

Rick's secretary stepped off the elevator and smiled at Lessa. Betty had worked at Lawrence for years and had been Rick's secretary ever since he had arrived. "Hello, Lessa," she said cheerfully.

Lessa felt a pang of guilt. Unlike her boss, Betty was kind and good-hearted. For some reason that Lessa couldn't fathom, she was also devoted to her boss. She knew Betty would be upset to hear that her longtime boss would not be working there anymore.

"What are you doing here so late?" Lessa asked.

"Rick had some research he wanted ASAP," Betty said, rolling her eyes. "Some people have no respect for the Christmas season. I've only got half of my shopping done. Have you started yet?"

Lessa was finished with her Christmas shopping only because there was just one person on her list—Gran. Almost eighty years old, Gran was her great-aunt, her only living relative and her best friend. Lessa had always been close to her aunt and had grown even closer after her father had died. Gran had been awarded custody and Lessa had moved into her small condo in a Florida retirement community. Years later, when her aunt sustained an injury, Lessa had repaid the favor, moving Gran into her New York apartment so that she could care for her. Although her aunt was healed and could have moved back into her old condo, Gran had made it clear that she liked staying with Lessa. And Lessa preferred it that way, too. After years of living by herself, it was nice to have some company. "I'm done with my shopping," Lessa said.

"Oh, lucky girl. How do you have time? You're here around the clock."

"The Internet."

"Ah. I still like to shop the old-fashioned way. I love being in stores during Christmas. There's an excitement in the air, don't you think?"

"Yes," Lessa said, suddenly realizing that she was still leaning up against Rick's door as if blocking Betty's path. She stepped away from the door and took Betty's hand. "I just want you to know that regardless of what happens to Rick, you have nothing to worry about." She would take care of Rick's secretary. The only person she planned on getting rid of was Rick. Leaving a confused Betty, she hurried to the elevator, stepping inside just as Betty opened her boss's door.

As the elevator doors closed, Lessa caught a glimpse of Rick. He was staring straight at her, and the look in his eyes gave her pause. It was not the look of a man who had just lost his job. It was a look of pity. Of regret.

But why would he feel sorry for her?

* * *

"That was odd," Betty said as she walked into the room. "I wonder what she meant by that."

Rick glanced at the stack of documents in her hand. "Is that my research?"

She nodded as she gave him the papers. "She said that no matter what happens to you, I don't have anything to worry about. Do you know what she was talking about?"

"I've just been fired," he said casually, thumbing through the documents.

"What?" she exclaimed, the surprise registering on her lined features. "That can't be."

"Alessandra has decided that she's ready to take over Lawrence Enterprises."

"That's ridiculous. She's too young."

"She's the same age her father was when he started the company."

"But you *are* the company. If it wasn't for you, the stock would be worthless."

"I don't think she realizes that. She feels that this is her rightful place. It was her father's company, therefore it's owed to her."

Betty sank into a chair, stunned. He used the momentary silence to his advantage, quickly scanning the document. It was a list of all the companies that had purchased Lawrence Enterprises stock in the past two weeks. Alessandra's mismanagement had weakened the company and the stock value considerably. Gossip surrounding the tension in his relationship with the chairman of the board of Lawrence Enterprises had been circulating for months. Industry insiders knew that

Rick's departure would make the company a prime target for a takeover. And, from the evidence before him, several ambitious corporate vultures were already hungrily gobbling up stock.

As he glanced over the names of the buyers, several in particular stood out. They were all companies owned by a woman he'd once dated, Sabrina Vickers. Sabrina owned many different companies, each under a different name. And there was only one reason she would be buying so much stock under all those different names: She didn't want anyone to know what she was up to. Sabrina, it appeared, was planning a hostile takeover of Lawrence Enterprises.

He had no doubt that Alessandra had scoured over this very same data, looking for signs of exactly this. But there's no way she could've figured it out yet.

In a small voice, Betty said, "I assume I'll be next?"

"I thought she just told you not to worry," he said.

"Don't worry? I've got two kids in college. I've worked here for the past thirty years. I can't imagine finding another job." She breathed in deeply and said, "Two weeks before Christmas and she's firing people. It's not right. You're going to fight her on this, aren't you, Rick?"

"Alessandra Lawrence is not gunning for anyone else. Believe me, she could barely fire me." He was an expert at reading his opponents. He had heard the hesitation in her voice and seen the anxiety in her eyes. At least, he thought, she had enough common sense to be frightened.

"Rick," she said, leaning on his desk, "what are you going to do?"

He glanced up, meeting her eyes directly. "Absolutely nothing. If Miss Lawrence wants this company, she's going to get it."

"But I thought you said I didn't have anything to worry about? We all know what's going to happen with her in charge. The stock's been plummeting ever since she became chairman of the board."

"I assume Alessandra thinks that it will all blow over once she proves herself."

"By the time she figures out what she's doing, there won't be any company left." Betty shook her head. "To think I knew her when she was just a girl. I remember her father bringing her to work. He was so proud of her. She was a big tennis player, remember?"

"Not really."

"She won the NCAA and a bunch of other competitions. Her matches were even on TV a couple times. We all thought she was going to turn pro. She was a nice girl, always so quiet and polite. She had such a crush on you back then. She used to hang around that drinking fountain right outside your office. You have to remember that, don't you?"

"I think you're mistaken, Betty." His memory of Howard Lawrence's daughter back from those days was foggy at best. The Alessandra Lawrence of today was a beautiful woman, with long, curly red hair and sparkling green eyes. He remembered when he'd first laid eyes on her after not seeing her for years. He'd had no idea who she was and couldn't help but feel an immediate attraction. She'd been dressed conservatively in a fitted green suit that outlined her lithe figure. His attraction for her had dimmed when he'd discovered that the office visitor was none other than Alessandra Lawrence. Even if she weren't the most insufferable woman he had ever met, he would never get involved with her. He had no intention of having an affair with the largest shareholder.

"Who would think that she would come back and destroy us all?" Betty shook her head.

"Let's not get carried away. The fight is hardly over. In fact, it's just beginning." He grinned. "Now go grab your briefcase. We're going to move operations to my apartment for a while."

After Betty left, Rick began packing files. He had expected this moment for quite a while. Although he had hoped that, for her sake, Alessandra would change her mind, he was not surprised. She had made it clear she was out for revenge from the first moment she had come into her stock. At the time, he had paid little attention. He knew she was attempting to get on the board, but he couldn't imagine the board would vote her on, much less hand her the chairmanship on a silver platter.

After all, what were her qualifications? A fancy degree and a couple of years experience at a rival firm. But the board had been sympathetic to her cause. She wanted to run the company her deceased parents had begun.

Unfortunately, everyone was overlooking the fact that it had not been Howard Lawrence's company for a very long time. It was Rick's blood and sweat that had made the company into what it was today. When he'd first started working at Lawrence, it had been a small firm, desperately in need of change. The woman he loved and planned to marry had just died, and Lawrence Enterprises offered him a chance to travel the world. For the first few months he functioned on automatic, working to escape his pain. And every time he returned to

New York, he couldn't wait to escape once more. He worked twenty hours a day. One month he'd be in South America, the next in Asia.

But his newfound peace was short-lived. Howard Lawrence soon took the company public and the new board was concerned that he was not capable of taking it to the next level. When they first approached Rick about taking it over, he was hesitant. He knew how much the company meant to his boss. But, as they reminded him, they had already made their decision. Howard Lawrence was out. Rick had assumed the presidency and all the trials and tribulations that came with it. He had paid a steep price, devoting one hundred percent of his time and energy to making it a success.

Not that he minded. He had not met anyone since Karen who had inspired him to miss a meeting in Singapore or a hotel opening in Rio. His family had grown used to him missing birthdays and holidays. But if Alessandra had her way, that would all change very soon.

It was not anger he felt, however, but pity. He was not about to be cast aside by a woman who had anointed herself heir apparent. He had no choice but to teach her a lesson she'd never learned in all of her graduate programs.

He was going to destroy her, Rick Parker style.

Two

If Lessa had expected an easy transition to CEO of Lawrence Enterprises, she would've been greatly disappointed. But she had been a competitive athlete, a top junior player with a big serve and an even bigger return of serve. And although she was used to charging out to a big lead, not every match went that way. She knew that no matter how many hours she spent on the court practicing, there were times when her serve would be off, or her return would be shaky, and her opponent would be the one in command. Then she'd have to play from behind. It wasn't her first choice, but in a way, it had been good for her. It proved to people she wasn't getting by on talent alone, that she could gut out a match with the best of them. Since she'd started at Lawrence Enterprises, she'd likened her struggle to a rough match. She might be in a hole, but she knew she'd dig herself out. Somehow.

But now, less than twenty-four hours after firing Rick Parker, she was beginning to think she had underestimated her opponent.

She had arrived at work that morning to find out that the company was under threat of a hostile takeover by Sabrina Vickers, heir to the Kato Resorts family fortune. Sabrina was known for taking over corporations and breaking them up, selling off the properties one by one. If she succeeded in taking over Lawrence Enterprises, the company would be ripped apart in a matter of months.

"You must be exhausted," her aunt said when Lessa finally made it home that night. "You've been at work since five this morning. And I bet you haven't had anything decent to eat all day." Her aunt shook her head as she walked over to their small galley kitchen. Their apartment was located on the top floor of a brownstone in midtown Manhattan. It was a simple two-bedroom with a living room and a small dining room. But it had one luxurious feature: an old, original wood-burning fireplace complete with a marble mantel. Lessa would often come home to find her dinner on the table and a roaring fire in the fireplace. Tonight, although it was nearly ten o'clock, was no exception.

Lessa pleaded with her aunt not to hold dinner for her, but her aunt was determined to do just that. "What else have I got to do all day?" she'd asked in her usual cranky tone.

"How could I not have seen this coming?" Lessa said after she told her aunt the news.

"She was too sneaky," Gran said.

Although Sabrina had bought stock through her various companies, never using her own name, Lessa blamed herself for not being more diligent. After all, she knew that a hostile takeover was a threat during any period of turmoil. "But she's been buying stocks for weeks. I should've been more thorough."

"Stop beating yourself up, Lessa. You know what your father always said. Don't waste time thinking about what you should've done. The question is, what can you do now?"

"The board wants me to bring back Rick." That was putting it mildly. Although the majority had voted to fire Rick, news of the takeover had sent her supporters running for cover. Everyone was pointing a finger and most were aimed directly at her. They considered Rick the one person capable of saving Lawrence Enterprises.

Her aunt sat down at the table and raised her eyebrows as if to say, "Well?"

"I've tried to call him to discuss it but he hasn't returned my calls." Lessa knew this was just part of his mind game, psyching out the opponent, but it still unnerved her. "You should've seen how smug he was last night. How cocky. I'm certain he knew about this takeover when I fired him. It was like…like he knew I would be forced to ask him back."

"So you've decided to give him back his job?" her aunt asked.

"I don't know what to do. I'd prefer to fight this myself. It could be an opportunity to win not only my company but the respect of everyone who works there."

"Sounds like a good idea. Now eat your dinner."

"Unfortunately," Lessa said after she dutifully took a bite, "the cons are enormous. I stand a very good chance of losing everything. I'm taking a gamble not only with my career but also with the livelihoods of everyone associated with Lawrence. If I lose, a lot of people will suffer." She didn't mind gambling with her own future, but she did not feel right risking the livelihoods of so many others.

"You think Rick can save the company?" her aunt asked.

"Maybe. He's well respected inside the company and in the industry. I think his presence alone would soothe stockholders." Once again she saw him standing in his office, his handsome blue eyes twinkling with arrogance. "Rick outplayed me. He'll get a new contract and be able to demand more money."

"*If* you take him back."

She set down her fork. "Oh, Gran, I've made a mess of things."

"Nonsense. I've never been more proud."

"How can you say that? Look what I've done. If Sabrina gets this company, she'll destroy it. She'll sell it off piece by piece."

"I hate to see you like this," her aunt said. "I don't think your father realized what a burden he presented you with."

"No," she said, shaking her head. "I was given a wonderful opportunity."

"Wonderful? Look at you. Twenty-six with the weight of the world on your shoulders and more than a thousand people's livelihood dependent on your decisions. It's Christmastime. You should be out celebrating with friends, drinking eggnog and kissing under the mistletoe. Instead you're staying up all night worrying about this company."

"Dad was my age when he began Lawrence. He had the same responsibilities."

"Your father was already married when he and your mother bought that old inn. And there was another big difference. This was his choice. His dream. It was your mother's dream as well."

"It's my dream too."

"Is it?" Her aunt sighed. "I loved your father dearly but sometimes I wish he was still here just so I could wring his neck. How could he do this to you?"

They had been over this so many times before. "Gran…"

"All I know was that he wasn't thinking straight. I know in my heart that he would not be happy to see that you had tossed aside your dreams just to fulfill his. No parent wants that for his child."

Lessa knew her father had loved her dearly. No one had been prouder of her tennis success than him. He had given her her first racket and had been her original coach. But things had changed after he'd taken the company public. She'd rarely seen him and when she had, he'd been too exhausted to do anything but read. She had been as surprised as anyone when he'd called her into his hospital room and had asked her to win back his company. But she had loved her father dearly and would've done anything to help him. She had made him a promise that she intended to keep. "But I like this business," Lessa said.

"Let's be honest," her aunt said. "If you hadn't made him that promise, would you be sitting here today fretting over the status of this company?"

Would she? She honestly didn't know. But it made

little difference. Lessa did not believe in wasting time thinking about what could have been. Her tennis career had ended long ago. Keeping Lawrence Enterprises out of the hands of Sabrina Vickers was what mattered now.

"I know I want this company to survive. More than I've ever wanted anything," she said.

"Then I have no doubt you'll succeed. You had the courage to go up against Rick Parker. Not many people would dare such a feat. Your father did, of course. And we all know what happened to him." Her aunt smiled. "You're a very determined girl. You always have been."

She smiled appreciatively. "Thanks, Gran. I don't know what I'd do without you."

Her aunt walked over to the kitchen counter and grabbed a small brown bag out of a cardboard box.

"What's this?" Lessa asked.

"It's a little something to cheer you up."

Lessa opened up the bag. "Mistletoe?"

"I thought it might help you enjoy the season."

"Thanks, Gran, but I don't think I'll be doing much kissing this Christmas."

"Both the Vikings and the druids believed there were special powers associated with mistletoe. That it was capable of miracles."

"You've been talking to Mr. Chapman again, haven't you?" Mr. Chapman was the owner of Chapman's Market, where they typically did their shopping. He was an amateur historian and every time Lessa's aunt went shopping, she returned home with a story. "It would be a miracle if I actually had someone to kiss this Christmas."

"Make a wish and we'll see if it comes true," Gran suggested.

Lessa laughed for the first time that day. "I wish for my own company. A successful company with employees who actually like me."

"Now it's my turn," her aunt said, taking the mistletoe and closing her eyes. She opened her eyes back up and said, "There."

"You're not going to tell me what you wished for?" Lessa asked.

Gran shook her head. "No. Now help me decide where I should hang this."

"How about in the closet?"

"Now, that's not optimistic of you."

Lessa smiled. She appreciated her aunt's enthusiasm. Usually, she loved Christmas, but this season was proving to be especially difficult. The stress of work was getting to her.

"What else is in that box?" Lessa asked, spying the small black writing on the side. As she walked toward it, the words came into focus: Christmas Ornaments. She suddenly remembered that she had promised to pick up a tree on her way home.

"We were supposed to have our tree-trimming party tonight," Lessa said apologetically. Every year she and her aunt celebrated the season by decorating the tree together. Lessa had been so distracted by work that she had completely forgotten.

"We'll do it another time."

"I'm sorry, Gran. I feel terrible. I know how much you were looking forward to putting up the tree."

"Oh, please," her aunt said, brushing it off. "I don't care about a silly tree. What I care about is you." Her aunt sighed. "I'm worried about you, Lessa. You're young and beautiful. There's no reason you shouldn't have someone to kiss under the mistletoe."

"Maybe next Christmas," she forced herself to say. She didn't want to disappoint her aunt but she knew the possibility of her having a boyfriend next Christmas was the same as it had been this year and the year before—slim to nil. As much as she might like to have someone special, it wasn't in the cards anytime soon. How could she get involved with someone when she typically worked thirteen hours a day, six or seven days a week? "Not this Christmas, I'm afraid." She absent-mindedly picked up the mistletoe as she thought once again about her situation at work. "This Christmas I'll be lucky to still have Lawrence Enterprises."

Her aunt sighed. "Well then, go do what you need to do. Go confront this Rick Parker in person."

"Go to his apartment?" She didn't like the idea of going to see him in such a personal location. She had been there once before, a decade earlier, when her father had sent her to deliver some files. She remembered how nervous she had been, remembered the way her heart had jumped into her throat when he answered the door. He had just returned from a trip and his shirt was untucked and halfway unbuttoned. Stubble of a beard along his jaw added to his dangerous charm.

Although Rick had been twenty-seven years old, eleven years her senior, she had fantasized about being invited inside. "I know you're young," he would say, "but I'm willing to wait." And then he would take her in his arms and give her a kiss she would remember for years. But in reality, he barely looked at her. He took the files and was perusing the information when she heard a woman laugh. She looked around Rick and saw a woman leaning against the couch. She was wearing a long, silky robe and thumbing through a magazine. She reminded Lessa of a gangster's moll, with tousled platinum-blond hair and bright pink lipstick. Rick had signed the papers and Lessa had left, feeling envious of the woman wearing the beautiful lingerie. Lessa thought her the luckiest woman in the world.

"I don't know that I can go there without an invitation."

"What choice do you have?" Gran asked.

Her aunt was right. She didn't have a choice. As much as she hated to admit it, she had a feeling the board was right. Only one man could save Lawrence Enterprises. Rick Parker.

Rick was not surprised to hear that Alessandra was waiting in his lobby. In fact, he had been expecting her. After all, forcing a personal meeting was exactly what he would've done under similar circumstances. What else was there to do when your nemesis refused your calls?

The truth of the matter was that he had been too busy to speak with her. His phone had been ringing all day. The stock had dropped significantly, and board members, furious with Alessandra, had been pleading with him to come back. But it wasn't the loquacious board that had prevented him from speaking to Alessandra. It was the fact that he himself was one of those gobbling up discarded stock for a discounted price—all under various business ventures, never his own name. By firing him, Alessandra had given him the power to do what, as CEO of Lawrence, he was legally forbidden—buy stock.

It was all part of his plan to regain power and rid himself of Alessandra Lawrence for once and for all. The plan was simple. He would purchase stock without Alessandra's knowledge. When she was forced to ask him back, he would negotiate a deal in which she gave him whatever stock he still needed for a majority. Once he had a majority, he could do whatever he liked. And his first order of business would be to fire Alessandra.

The elevator doors opened and Alessandra stepped into his apartment. He had to give her credit. In spite of the hellish day he knew she must have suffered, she looked remarkably composed. Her long red hair was pulled back in a ponytail and she was wearing a gray overcoat. She held her head up high, making her look like a regal queen who was blessing him with her presence.

"Hello," he said as she walked toward him. "This is a surprise."

"Is it?" she replied, meeting his gaze directly. "I would've assumed that you knew very well this meeting would happen."

He held back a grin as he motioned toward the couch. "Please," he said.

"What are your terms?" she asked quietly, standing right where she was.

"Terms?"

"I'm not here to play games, Rick. I assume you knew about the hostile takeover. You orchestrated your own firing yesterday simply to terminate your contract in the midst of a corporate upheaval. You knew that I would be forced to rehire you on your own terms."

"And are you?" He knew better than to waste his time

by attempting to deny the accusations. She wouldn't believe him anyway. And he cared little what she thought.

She snapped open her briefcase. "I'm prepared to give you a ten-percent raise and a one-year extension on your contract."

She handed him the contract but he didn't accept it. "I'm not interested."

"What do you mean?"

He could hear the nervousness in her voice and see the fear in her eyes. Without realizing it, she was giving away her hand. She knew she needed him.

"Ten percent and a one-year extension are not enough."

She swallowed, taking a deep breath. "What do you want?"

"I want the raise, the extension, and…" He paused, noticing the way the her slender hands clutched the papers. "Half of your stock."

The color drained from her face. No wonder. It was an outrageous request. So outrageous that he had not even pondered it. But since she seemed so desperate to have him return, why not?

"No," she said.

He took another step toward her. He was so close, he could smell her slight flowery scent. "Well then," he said in a soft whisper, "I don't think we have anything to talk about."

Her eyes were full of fire as she tightened her lips. "This was my father's company. He always intended that I would one day be at the helm."

"And maybe you will. In the meantime, I'll own half of your stock. We'll be partners."

"Partners?" she asked quietly, her voice ragged.

It was obvious that she was hesitant to give up hope that she might one day regain the company. But it was difficult to feel pity for her naïveté. She should've known better than to challenge him. He had warned her and she had no one but herself to blame for the consequences.

Still, this interaction was making him uncomfortable. He would have an easier time of this if she were defiant and narcissistic. He walked back toward the elevator and pressed the button. As the doors opened he said, "Feel free to take some time to think about my offer. But the bottom line will not change. You need me if you're going to save your father's company. You and I both know I'm the only one capable of accomplishing this. If I don't come back, try as you might, I can guarantee you that Sabrina Vickers will take over the company. And when she does, she will do what she has always done. She will break it up into little pieces, selling off the properties your father and I have worked so hard to build. By next year Lawrence Enterprises will be nothing but a memory. Is that what your father would have wanted?"

He could almost see the inner machinations of her brain. She had no choice but to accept his terms, however audacious they were. "I've worked very hard for this company, Alessandra. I've given it fifteen years of my life. I don't want to see it destroyed. But this is your decision."

"I'll agree under one condition," she said after a moment's hesitation. "That I give you my shares only when the threat of a takeover is alleviated."

"Fine," he said, holding out his hand. "So we have a deal."

"I'm willing to put past grievances behind us in order to save the company," she said. With what appeared to be a supreme amount of effort, she accepted his hand.

"I'm very happy to hear that, Lessa," he said, squeezing her hand gently. "Because in order to save this company, you're going to have to forget what you learned in grad school. Now," he said, letting go of her hand, "can I take your coat?"

"What do you mean, forget what I learned?" she asked, shrugging off her coat and handing it to him.

"Sabrina Vickers is simply the first in a long line of companies waiting to steal Lawrence Enterprises," he said, hanging up her coat. "The problem is not Sabrina, it's the perception that Lawrence Enterprises is a company in turmoil. All the Sabrinas have crawled out of the woodwork. And there's only one way to get rid of them."

"Let's hear it," she said, taking a seat on his leather sofa.

He sat across from her and leaned forward. "We need to convince Sabrina and everyone else that my job is intact. That our…union is secure."

"What are you suggesting?"

He paused, almost enjoying the look of anticipation in her eyes. "We're lovers."

He watched as the surprise in her eyes gave way to indignation.

"No," she said.

"Just for show, of course. It's the only way. We need to prove to Sabrina Vickers and the rest of the world that we're together. That my firing was simply a lovers' quarrel. If you and I are united, in both power and money, they'll know better than to attempt another takeover."

"That's ridiculous," she said, standing. "This is business, not make-believe."

He stood up so that he was towering over her. "If Sabrina thinks for one moment that you asked me back only because of her takeover bid, she's going to know that my stay is only temporary. She'll know that, sooner or later, you're going to fire me again. The end result is that she will never give up her shares. She will simply wait it out and strike when the timing is right."

"This ridiculous scenario is the best you can offer? I don't think so. We'll win this company back the old-fashioned way. By proving that we're stronger than her."

"But we're not. In the past year, stocks have fallen considerably. Stockholders are aware of the turmoil at Lawrence and are anxious to shed their shares while they're still worth something. You got us into this mess, Miss Lawrence. I think you owe it to everyone to do whatever you can to get us out." He could almost see the disdain in her emerald eyes.

"What does this…plan of yours entail?" she asked.

"We meet with Sabrina and do our best to convince her that we're in love…or at least, you're in love with me. We'll explain my departure as your reaction to a lovers' quarrel. That you would never really do anything to harm me or the company."

"I'm not an actress, Mr. Parker. And I'm not a hysterical woman." He didn't doubt it. She looked as icy as princesses come. But beneath the veneer he could swear he saw something else. Perhaps, he thought, she was one of those women whose prim visage was a mask for the fire and passion beneath.

"How long will it take you to draw up the contract?" he asked.

"I have to have it approved by the board first."

"That shouldn't be a problem. Meet me at Teterboro Airport tomorrow at eight in the morning. Bring the contract with you. I'll sign it before we leave."

"But that's less than ten hours from now."

"I guess you should get going, then," he said, taking her coat out of the closet.

"I have not agreed to do this."

"You'll do it, Miss Lawrence. You have no choice." As he hung her coat around her shoulders, his fingers brushed the skin of her creamy-white neck. She jerked forward, touching her fingers to the spot as if burned.

Her eyes narrowed and he could see the hatred burning inside. She took a step toward him and for a moment he thought she might slap him. Finally she bit her lower lip and turned away with her head held high, as regal in defeat as she was in victory. He couldn't help but smile as he shut the door.

He was going to enjoy this.

Three

Lessa sat beside Rick in the limo, determined to maintain her composure. She forced herself to focus on the laptop screen before her, trying to forget that she and Rick were getting closer to Sabrina Vickers by the minute. That Rick had just signed a deal in which she gave him half her stock, essentially making them partners, paled in comparison to the task at hand. But she had no choice. After all, to bow out was to admit defeat. And she was not defeated. Not yet anyway.

She had, however, suffered a professional setback that was so severe many at the office were already planning her retirement. The rumor mill had been working overtime ever since she'd arrived. Everyone knew she would not be the chairman or even on the board if she didn't own a majority stake in the company. The most recent rumor had her paying off the board members to

get her post. Her efforts to win the employees over—
starting a day care in the office, increasing benefits,
even supplying coffee and doughnuts in the morning—
were ignored.

Time, she reminded herself. She needed to be patient.
After all, her father had been just as beloved as Rick.
Rick had had to work hard to turn the tide of sympathy,
but he had done such a good job that the employees
seemed to have forgotten all about her father. The fact
that she was Howard Lawrence's daughter and the rightful heir to Lawrence Enterprises meant little. The only
thing that mattered from now on was how well she got
along with Rick.

They were no longer opponents but partners. Her
new strategy revolved around winning Rick's respect.
She had a hunch that if she won Rick over, she might be
able to win over everyone else. It was a strategy that held
little appeal, but she had no choice. She had made a deal
with the devil and now she had to make the best of it.

Lessa glanced at Rick. He was talking on his cell
phone, laughing as he spoke to a colleague. The crin-
kles from his laugh lines only made him look more
handsome. Wearing an open-neck business shirt and
khaki slacks, he looked relaxed and in control, totally
at ease with the caper they were about to attempt.

Once again panic gripped her heart as she thought,
What am I doing?

Could she really pull this off? What did he have in
mind? Holding hands and kissing? Or just exchanging
knowing glances?

She took a deep breath and closed her eyes. She had
to approach this just as she would a tough match. Like

the one she'd played against Korupova, the tall Russian girl with the black hair, in the NCAAs her sophomore year. Korupova was a lauded champion and Lessa began the match determined that the only way to win was to hit every bit as hard as her opponent. But it soon became obvious that she was outmatched. Korupova was a better and stronger athlete. Since Lessa could not win the match on the strength of her strokes, she had to come up with a new strategy. She switched from offensive playing to defensive, hoping that through sheer determination and patience she could outlast her opponent. In the end, Lessa had squeaked out a victory. She counted that win as the best of her career because it made her think she could get into something completely over her head and somehow, someway, get her feet under her and win. Just like now. Rick may be a superior player, but by staying in the moment, by not letting her fears get the best of her, she would get her feet under her again. And she would be victorious.

"Are you ready?" he asked, snapping his phone shut.

She glanced at him and nodded.

He smiled and took her hand. His touch sent a bolt of electricity running through her. So surprised was she by her reaction to him that she yanked her hand away.

"Now, now, Lessa," he said, purposely referring to her by her nickname. "Is that a way to respond to a lover's touch?" He shook his head, still holding her captive with his eyes. She couldn't miss the twinkle of mischief there. It was obvious he took pleasure in her discomfort. She was certain it was a different experience than what he was used to. When he held a woman's hand, he probably expected a sigh of delight.

"I suggest you swallow back whatever revulsion you feel toward me and focus," he said sternly. "When I touch you, do not grimace or make an effort to get away. Remember your mission and do your job."

He was right. She had agreed to this; now she had no choice but to give it her all. After all, if they were successful with Sabrina, they could single-handedly thwart all other takeover attempts. Maybe. At the very least, they could buy themselves some time to prevent this from happening again. She took a deep breath and picked up his hand. Still staring into his eyes, she brought his hand to her mouth and kissed it.

His eyes softened and he smiled. "That's better," he said. "I knew you could do it if you put your mind to it." Then he pulled his hand away and opened his cell phone, making another call and going back to business as if nothing had happened.

She rolled down the shaded limousine window, welcoming the bright sunshine. They were meeting Sabrina at one of her most famous resorts. Located on Paradise Island in the Bahamas, it was one of the most romantic resorts in the world, catering to honeymooners. Lessa breathed in the warm, tropical air. New York had been dark and overcast with the forecast of another day of freezing rain. She reminded herself that this was one of the things her parents had loved about this business. Whenever one world became unpleasant, they could escape to another.

She kept reminding herself how fortunate she was as the car pulled into the gated resort and stopped in front of a large bungalow marked Executive Offices.

"Wait for me to open your door," Rick instructed,

purposely tucking his collar under his jacket. "When we get out, I want you to adjust my shirt collar. After that, follow my lead."

He walked around the car and opened her door. He took her hand and helped her out, pulling her close. What, she couldn't help but wonder, was the point of this playacting before they even saw Sabrina? Did he think that she was spying on them from a window? Or was it just for rehearsal's sake? Despite her hesitation, Lessa did as she was instructed, carefully adjusting his collar. When she was finished, Rick smiled and put his arm around her, guiding her to the door. His arm weighed against her back as they walked. To be so close to him felt strange, but, surprisingly, not uncomfortable. In fact, there was something sensual about the way he held her, as if he were publicly claiming her as his.

The secretary led them into a large, airy office with overstuffed furniture upholstered in tropical prints. When a statuesque woman stood behind a desk, Lessa stopped in her tracks. Blond, busty and completely made-up, she was the same woman Lessa had seen that night in Rick's apartment. And suddenly the cold, hard truth hit her like a slap on the face. It was she, not Sabrina, who was being duped.

"Rick," Sabrina said. She held out her hands, signaling him to greet her.

What was going on? As Lessa watched Rick walk toward Sabrina, her heart banged against her chest so hard she was certain they both could hear.

Sabrina took his hands and kissed him on both cheeks. Without letting go, she said, "It's been too long."

How could he do this? Lessa thought. *How could he have pretended not to know who Sabrina was?*

Rick stepped back from Sabrina, as if suddenly remembering his date. "Sabrina, this is Alessandra Lawrence," he said.

"Well, well," Sabrina said, giving Lessa a careful once-over. "She's a beautiful girl, Rick."

"You two know each other," Lessa said coldly.

Sabrina smiled. "Rick and I are old friends."

"I've met you before," Lessa said. "At Rick's apartment." Rick glanced at her, startled. "I seem to remember that you two were more than just friends."

"We were lovers," Sabrina said, flashing her a pearly white smile. "Rick? You didn't tell Alessandra about me?" she teased. "I'm insulted."

Rick looked Lessa in the eye and said, "Sabrina and I haven't seen each other in years."

"Has it been that long?" Sabrina said. "It seems like only yesterday." She turned back toward Lessa and said, "We spent Christmas together one year."

Lessa couldn't take her eyes off Rick. Had he set this whole thing up? Was the whole "takeover" staged simply so that he could get his job back? As tempted as she was to confront him right there and then, she couldn't risk it. What if was just an awful coincidence? After all, she knew Rick had engaged in many affairs. Perhaps Sabrina was just another one of his women.

"We've come to make you an offer," Lessa said, glaring at Rick. She wanted to get this over as soon as possible.

"She's all business, isn't she?" Sabrina asked him.

"She's determined."

Why were they talking about her as if she weren't there?

"As Rick will attest," Lessa said, flashing him a smile, "I don't believe in wasting time."

"Something else we have in common," Sabrina said.

Something else? Lessa had nothing in common with the overly made-up, phony woman standing across from her.

Sabrina motioned toward the chairs and took a seat on the couch across from them.

"I don't mean to pry, Rick," Sabrina said, "but I was a bit surprised to get your phone call yesterday. After all, I had heard that you weren't working at Lawrence anymore."

"Reports of my demise were greatly exaggerated," he said.

"Were they?" She focused her black eyes on Lessa. "I had heard that Alessandra fired you."

"A lovers' quarrel gone public," he said, putting his hand on Lessa's bare knee.

"Really?" Sabrina crossed her arms and leaned back in her chair. "So you and Alessandra are…together, shall we say?"

Rick nodded. "For some time now. Of course, we've been hesitant to take our affair public, for obvious reasons."

"And she got mad and fired you. Tsk, tsk, Rick. What did you do to deserve such treatment?"

"It was all a misunderstanding," he said, giving Lessa a squeeze.

Sabrina's lip curled up suspiciously, as if she didn't believe him. "Very vindictive of you, Alessandra. Not to mention stupid. You should've been aware that firing him would make your company vulnerable."

How dare she? "I was acting under—"

Rick gave her knee a light squeeze and she knew he was signaling her to be careful. "I wasn't thinking very clearly at the time," Lessa said, doing her best not to take Sabrina's bait. "And it cost me dearly." *Very dearly,* she felt like adding.

Sabrina said nothing; she merely glanced at Rick.

"She's a very passionate woman," he said with a shrug. "For better or worse."

"And I remember how much you enjoy passion," Sabrina said, giving him a little smile.

Lessa couldn't stop herself from sending Rick a look of her own, an angry one.

"Oh dear, Rick," Sabrina continued. "It looks like she's not very happy with you. I certainly hope I didn't cost you your job again." Sabrina laughed. It was a cold, empty sound, just as haunting as Lessa remembered.

But the laugh was enough to remind her of her mission. Pretending to be Rick's lover was bad enough. She would not play the weak and hurt mistress. "Oh, no," Lessa said. "It's just difficult for me to keep all of Rick's old lovers straight. In fact, when I first heard about your takeover attempt, I assumed it was the move of a bitter ex-girlfriend. You know, retribution for his new romance."

The smiled faded from Sabrina's lips. "She's very spirited, Rick. I can see why she caught your eye. Although she looks a little buttoned-up for you."

Buttoned up? "I'm losing my patience," Lessa said, standing. Rick took her arm and raised his eyebrow, motioning for her to sit. She knew that he was right. She had no choice but to continue.

When she was seated, Rick turned to Sabrina. "The

bottom line is that the situation is not what you thought. I am not leaving Lawrence Enterprises."

"You can't defeat both of us," Lessa added.

"So my purchasing stock was enough to heal a..." Sabrina glanced at Rick. "How did you describe it? A lovers' quarrel? Perhaps you should be thanking me, Rick, for winning back your job."

"Let's face it, Sabrina, If not you, it would've been someone else."

"If I remember correctly, there was someone else," Sabrina snapped. "There were several in fact."

Was she implying that he'd been unfaithful when they'd been seeing each other? Lessa wondered.

"Let's hear your offer," Sabrina said.

"We're willing to buy back your stock at a decent premium," Lessa explained as Rick opened his briefcase and handed Sabrina the contract.

After scanning the document, she put it on her desk. "Why should I agree to this when I could have all the properties?"

Rick leaned forward. "Because you're never going to get all the properties."

"I'm not so sure. You two seem to have a tumultuous relationship, to say the least. One that is not having positive repercussions on the company. Your stock has dropped rather dramatically."

"Actually," Lessa said, "when you look at our revenues in the context of the economy, we had an excellent year. And Rick has some properties due to open that should dramatically increase our value. But then again, you know our property is valuable, otherwise you wouldn't want it so badly."

Sabrina hesitated and glanced down at the contract. "I'll need some time to discuss this with my advisers. Unfortunately, they're out of the office right now, inspecting some properties. Perhaps, if you're not in a rush, you could stay until dinner. They'll be back by then and we can all discuss this further."

Lessa felt her heart stop. As excited as she was to think that perhaps Sabrina would abort the takeover, she couldn't bear the thought of carrying on this charade any longer than necessary.

"We would be happy to," Rick said, glancing at Lessa. The look in his eyes was clear. *Don't blow this.*

"It's settled," Sabrina said. "We have a couple of hours to play before we return to business. I'll have my secretary show you to your room. Why don't you change into your suits and meet me at the boat docks? I know how Rick loves to water-ski."

Water-ski? "Unfortunately," Lessa said quickly, "we didn't bring suits."

"I'll have some sent to your room."

Her heart jumped into her throat. Room? As in one room, not two? "It's not necessary," she said quickly. "We'll just pick some up at the gift shop."

"The gift shop is closed temporarily. Renovations," Sabrina said with a shrug.

"Well then, thank you," Lessa managed to say.

Rick took her arm and they followed the secretary, Christa, outside and down a palm-shrouded walkway. Beyond the walkway was a white sandy beach framed by the Caribbean. Christa stopped at a bungalow just feet away from the crystal-blue water. Their quarters were isolated from the rest, a special little love nest next to the sea.

Christa slid a card through a lock and opened the door. "Enjoy," she said cheerfully, handing Rick the card.

It was an opulent and meticulously appointed suite, with French doors that were open to the sea. A bottle of champagne sat chilled in an ice bucket, while two plush robes lay across a bed.

Lessa shut the doors and turned to face him. Her eyes were cold, her face set in a frown. "I thought you didn't like games."

"If you have a problem, Lessa, I suggest you tell me about it. I don't like dissent in the office."

"You know Sabrina Vickers?"

"I knew her," he said.

"Why didn't you tell me she was your girlfriend?" she asked. The accusations once again filled her head. Was he working with Sabrina? Was this all a joke? Had he arranged this just to get his job back? Was this just a ploy to get her stock?

"She was never a girlfriend."

"If she wasn't your girlfriend, then why did she insinuate that you cheated on her?"

"I don't see how that's any of your business."

"It most certainly is my business. Your girlfriend is threatening to take over my company and—"

"Your company?"

This conversation was going nowhere fast. He should at least be able to admit that he had made a mistake. "You should've told me this before."

"Would it have made any difference? I would think if anything, it would've made you more eager to retain my services. After all, I have firsthand knowledge of how to handle her."

The look in his eyes was of a confident victor. She had been deceived and he was enjoying every moment.

"Look," he said, his tone softening, "my relationship with Sabrina was casual. It lasted for a couple of days in Acapulco and then we got together a couple of times when she was in New York for business. Like I said, I haven't seen or spoken with her in years. But I do know that she is one of the toughest and smartest women I have ever met."

Lessa felt a tingle of...what? Jealousy? Why would she care if he thought that bubble-headed blonde with the beautiful lingerie and sexy laugh was intelligent? "You and I both know that I would not have asked you back if she wasn't threatening a takeover," Lessa said. "Do you expect me to believe that this is some sort of coincidence?"

"You're welcome to believe whatever you want. I would suggest, however, that you at least listen to the truth."

"And the truth is..."

"Exactly as I told her. If she hadn't attempted a takeover, someone else would've. This company is weaker than it's ever been. When a twenty-six-year-old with only two years of experience uses her father's connections to take over a company, the sharks start circling."

"I'm more capable than you give me credit."

"Maybe," he said. "Yet here I am."

"The question is why am *I*? Why didn't you just go see her yourself, considering your past relationship?"

"Whatever Sabrina and I shared has nothing to do with this. I know her well enough to realize that she cares little about our past relationship. She's only inter-

ested in making money. You're with me because we
need to convince her that we're a united front. The heir
to the Lawrence fortune and the man who has given you
his fortune are friends. If she suspects our relationship
is not sincere, she will never accept a deal. She will simply wait and strike again."

He shook his head and absentmindedly ran his fingers through his hair, as if frustrated. "Look, Lessa, as
I told you last night, the only one for you to blame for
this mess is yourself. Sabrina never would've attempted
this if I were in charge. You should've spent more time
doing your homework. If you did, you would've realized that any corporate upheaval makes a company ripe
for this sort of thing."

There was a knock on the door. Rick opened it and
accepted the package, handing the man a tip in exchange.
Rick looked inside the bag, and, with a wicked smile,
pulled out the tiniest swimsuit Lessa had ever seen.

She whipped it away from him. "She didn't by
chance include a cover-up in there, did she?"

He opened the bag again. It was clear he was enjoying this. "Not unless you want to wear this," he said,
pulling out his bathing-suit trunks.

She went in the bathroom and slammed the door. She
was fuming as she looked at the bright yellow string bikini. It was the type of suit guaranteed to get attention,
one that left little to the imagination. She slipped it on,
afraid to look at herself in the mirror. She knew without looking that her underwear covered more turf than
the suit. She had always been extremely modest, pre-
ferring swimsuits that covered her essentials and then
some. She wrapped a towel around her waist and, after

a moment's hesitation, opened the door. She hurried past Rick without looking at him. "Let's go," she said, heading outside.

"Wait." He grabbed her arm. "Sabrina might think you don't care," he said, tormenting her with his teasing tone.

She hesitated and he let go of her. He had changed into his bathing suit as well. She was not surprised to see that he had the physique of a natural athlete, finely sculpted and strong.

He gave her body a raking gaze. She pretended not to notice his obvious examination and approval, but she could feel her cheeks grow warm. "Take my hand," he instructed. His hands were large, swallowing hers. He could crush her, but instead he held her as gently as he could. "Take your time," he instructed. "Slowly. Don't forget, I'm your lover, not your enemy."

"It's easy to forget," she said.

His eyes gazed over her once again, slowly drinking her in. She could smell Rick, feel his presence.

"Let's get on with this," she said. She found herself thinking once again of Sabrina. She had done a lot more than just admire Rick's muscles. While Lessa had been worshipping him from afar, Sabrina had been experiencing his skills as a lover. She had no doubt Rick was as skilled at lovemaking as he was everything else.

"I'm curious about one thing," Rick said. "When did you see me with Sabrina?"

"At your apartment," she replied, not intending the words to sound as bitter as they did. "About ten years ago. My dad sent me over to deliver some papers."

"That was a long time ago," he said. "I'm surprised you even remember."

Of course she remembered, she felt like saying. She had been madly, wildly in love with him. But before she could say anything, his hand settled on top of her rear end. She could feel herself grow short of breath as he pulled her to a stop. "Sabrina is behind you," he said. "She's watching us."

He brushed the back of his hand across her face. "I'm going to kiss you, Lessa," he said quietly. "It's going to be a tender, passionate kiss. I want you to take your hands and wrap them around my neck. Can you do that?"

Oh God, oh God...

"Just relax," he said softly. "I'm not going to hurt you."

As he leaned forward, she closed her eyes and puckered up. His lips pressed against hers as his hand slipped around her small waist, pulling her in to him. As her bare flesh pressed against his, she was overwhelmed by his physical strength and power.

Slowly, he stopped. He smiled softly, his eyes caressing her. And for a moment, she forgot it was not real. He loved her and she loved him and that was all that mattered.

But instead of sweet nothings, he said, "You didn't put your arms around my neck." With a nod toward Sabrina, he added, "Next time follow instructions."

Four

"As I told you, Mr. Parker," Lessa said, still shaky from the kiss. "I'm not an actress."

"Well, you better try. Because this is the only way to get back your father's business. So no more tantrums." He swung her back into him.

"Every time you touch me, it makes me dislike you even more."

"Well, if all goes according to plan," he said, pulling her so close she could feel his breath on her cheek, "by the end of the evening you'll hate me." He released her but still held on to her hand. "Shall we?"

The afternoon sun reflected off the blue Caribbean, beating through the palm trees that flanked the path. They made their way to the white sandy beach toward a waving Sabrina. Lessa was surprised to see that Sabrina was wearing a suit even skimpier than hers.

"This way," Sabrina called out cheerfully.

Lessa glanced sideways at Rick. If Sabrina was wearing the bikini to impress him, it didn't appear to work. He was looking intently at Lessa. "Showtime," he told her softly.

"Well," Sabrina said, the smile fading from her face as she saw Lessa, "I see you got the suit. Who knew you had a figure underneath those big, bulky clothes of yours?"

"Lessa's in great shape," Rick said, smiling at her proudly. Lessa couldn't help but wince at the discussion of her physical attributes. She tightened the towel around her waist.

"She's a competitive tennis player," Rick said. "She even played at Wimbledon."

"The Wimbledon Juniors," Lessa corrected him, embarrassed by the exaggeration.

"How impressive," Sabrina said, obviously unimpressed. "But does she water-ski?"

Why did Sabrina insist on talking to Rick as if Lessa weren't there? "No, she doesn't," Lessa said, referring to herself in the third person.

"Oh, that's too bad," Sabrina said, with mock sincerity. "Perhaps you'd like to stay here and settle into a beach chair. We won't be long, will we, Rick?" Once again, she flashed her pearly whites.

"I'm always up for trying something new," Lessa said as enthusiastically as she could.

Rick jumped on the boat and held out his hand. She made herself take his hand and climbed onboard.

The boat took off and Sabrina fell against Rick. "Whoa," she said. Rick steadied her as Sabrina smiled at him gratefully. And that was when it hit Lessa. Sabrina was not only an ex-girlfriend, she was vying to be the current one as well. But did she really like him? Or was she, as Rick maintained, just trying to determine his response? After all, what better way to see if his relationship with Lessa was real?

As if thinking the same thing, Rick moved behind Lessa and slipped his arm around her shoulders. She glanced up at him and he smiled back.

"Does the rest of your office know what you're up to?" Sabrina asked, staring at them intently.

"No," Lessa said.

"Yes," Rick said, at exactly the same time.

He squeezed her shoulders again and said, "They didn't for a long time, but due to the most recent issue—"

"When I fired him," Lessa added cheerfully.

"It's become obvious that something is going on."

"I see." Sabrina said, picking up a bottle of sunscreen. She squirted some in her hand and stretched out one of her long legs, swinging it up and over the side of the boat. In a scene worthy of an X-rated film, she began slowly to smooth the lotion over her leg. It was obvious that Sabrina was doing some performing of her own. When she was done, she looked at Rick and said, "Lotion?"

He turned to Lessa and asked, "Would you mind putting some on my back?"

His back? "No," Lessa said, taking the lotion. She squirted some on her hands and forced herself to touch his bare skin. His skin was smooth and his back was outlined with well-formed muscles. She dug in deep, running her fingers against the muscles that seemed to grow hard with her touch. It was sensual and intimate, not the type of activity one would normally perform with a business associate. But she could not allow herself to feel embarrassed. Sabrina was watching.

"Thanks," he said huskily, as Sabrina signaled the boat's driver to stop. "You've got quite a touch," he added, giving her a mischievous grin.

Sabrina handed Rick a life jacket and said, "Why don't you go first." She helped it on him, making a point of rubbing in some lotion that was on his shoulder. "You missed a spot," she said, smiling evilly at Lessa.

Lessa couldn't help but resent the blatantly flirtatious act. If Rick really were her boyfriend, she would be fuming right now.

"Thanks," he said, then plunged into the water.

"Don't forget your ski," Lessa said, tossing it in. He moved out of the way just in time to avoid being clobbered. "So sorry, darling," she said.

Rick slipped on the ski and gave them the thumbs-up sign. He easily got up on the first try, all of his muscles taut.

Sabrina clapped her hands before focusing her attention back on Lessa. As Lessa watched Rick ski in and out of the wake, Sabrina said, "Rick and I met on a ski boat. It was very romantic. I took a bad tumble and had to be carried off the boat. Naturally Rick volunteered. All the other men, including my date, were sitting on the boat sipping their drinks. Well, that was that."

Lessa nodded. What was she supposed to do? She had the feeling that Sabrina was testing her, but what could she say? "Rick is a very gallant man."

"I take it you two met at work," Sabrina stated.

"I met Rick when he came to work for my father." Lessa could still see Rick standing before her, with his hair slicked back and his deep blue eyes, resplendent in an expensive suit. She remembered the feeling that had surged through her, a primitive need and desire so great she felt as if she might wilt away if he didn't love her in return. "I fell in love with Rick the first moment I saw him. Of course, he didn't know that," she said. And suddenly, she wasn't acting anymore. It was a true story, and recalling it now, after all these years, she could still feel the dull ache of longing for her old crush. "I was only fifteen and I don't think he even knew I existed. But I was so infatuated with him. I used to think of excuses to go to work with my dad just to see Rick. There was a drinking fountain right outside his office. I spent hours at that fountain."

"Love at first sight," Sabrina said sarcastically. "How sweet. So there's a significant age difference."

"Not really. About eleven years. Rick was pretty young when he started. It's one of those age differences that grows smaller and smaller through the years."

They glanced back but Rick was no longer there. Oops. Lessa was so into recalling her past love that she had forgotten to keep an eye on him.

"Turn it around," Sabrina said to the driver, pointing to a dot on the horizon.

They went back to Rick and he climbed back onto the boat. "You looked great out there," Sabrina said.

He nodded toward the towel, as if hinting at Lessa to get it. She jumped up and snatched it away just as Sabrina got up. "Thanks, babe," he said casually.

Babe. He called her *babe.* She had never liked that term of endearment. Macho slang for *baby,* it radiated sex.

He eyed them both and said, "What have you girls been talking about?"

"It was so sweet. Alessandra was telling me how she loved you at first sight. How she used to spend hours at the drinking fountain outside your office, just hoping for a smile from you." And with that, Sabrina touched his cheek. "It seems as if you were just too irresistible." Sabrina took a life preserver and fastened it on.

"Is that true?" he asked Lessa, looking at her quizzically.

"It was a long time ago," she said. "I was a kid."

Neither said anything else as Sabrina jumped into the water and put on her ski. As the boat took off, Rick wrapped his arm around Lessa, holding her tightly against him. They were flesh to flesh. She felt the movement of his breathing, the dampness of his skin. This was a little too close for comfort. She scooted away as she pretended to get a better look at Sabrina. She looked like a true professional gliding across the water with one ski. And then she began to show off, turning around backward and forward, smiling and waving at Rick. "She's good, isn't she?" Lessa remarked.

But Rick wasn't looking at Sabrina. He was looking at Lessa. There was something lazily seductive in his eyes, as though he were thoroughly enjoying the moment.

"I think Sabrina is still interested in you," Lessa said.

"No. We were together a long time ago. Besides, Sabrina's not the type to fall in love."

She raised an eyebrow. Women's intuition said differently.

When Sabrina was done, Rick leaned over the boat and helped her out of the water.

"Would you like to go again, Rick?" she asked as she stood in front of him, stretching every which way to pat herself dry.

Oh no, Lessa told herself, this was not how this was going to work, with her sitting on the sidelines watching Sabrina and Rick show off. "I'd like to give it a try," she announced.

"Good for you," Sabrina said in a patronizing tone. "She's got some spirit, Rick." She nodded toward the water. "Jump in and I'll throw you another ski."

"What's wrong with the one you both used?"

"It's easier if you get up on two skis," Rick said.

Out of the corner of her eye, she saw Sabrina smirk, as if mocking her.

"I'll do one," Lessa said.

"Take another ski," Rick said firmly.

No thanks. They did one, and so would she. "Don't worry, dear," she said, jumping into the water. She waded over toward the ski and attempted to put it on. But the boot was set for Sabrina's tiny size-five feet. Her size nines didn't stand a chance.

She struggled with the latch and glanced up. There was no mistaking the evil gleam in Sabrina's eyes. Then Lessa heard a splash as Rick jumped in the water. She couldn't help but feel relief as he swam over to help.

"It's stuck," she said, handing him the ski. He looked at her and said softly, "What's the deal? Why won't you use two skis?"

Why? Because his girlfriend had only used one. And she was…being silly?

"It seemed more convenient," she lied.

She tried to ignore Rick's disbelieving look as he called out, "Toss in another ski."

Sabrina threw it and it landed in the water beside them, barely missing Lessa's head. "Hey," Rick yelled. "Be careful!"

Rick adjusted the skis to fit her. "Hold on to me," he said. Lessa reluctantly put her arms around his neck to steady herself as he slid the skis on her feet. "You don't have to do this," he said.

"I want to do this," she said adamantly, letting go of him.

"All right," he said finally. "It's a little choppy so stay in the wake."

The wake. She got it. She could do this, she told herself. She had won the NCAAs, won the Wimbledon Juniors. She could certainly handle a little waterskiing. How hard could it be?

Rick climbed back on the boat. What had gotten into her? He knew Sabrina had been trying hard to goad her into action, but Lessa was too smart to let Sabrina get to her.

He was impressed with the way Lessa was handling herself. She was doing a good job of playing the concerned lover. He had been surprised at the sensuous way she had applied the lotion, massaging his shoulders and leaning close enough for him to feel her breasts pressing up against him. She had been effective. So effective that his body had sprung to life—a fact that Sabrina, with her eagle eyes and ability to read men, no doubt noticed.

But hell, who could blame him? After all, Lessa was half-naked in that bikini. Every ounce of her firm and toned body was exposed. It was all he could do to keep from staring at her large, upturned breasts, at her slender, perfect hips.

"She's ready," Sabrina said, telling the driver to go. The boat jolted to a start and Rick watched with dismay as Lessa flew out of the water and onto her head.

"Cut the engine," he yelled and jumped in, prepared to retrieve an unconscious woman from the water.

But she poked her head up. "I almost had it," she yelled out cheerfully.

"That's enough," he said sternly, swimming toward her. "Let's go in."

"I'm not about to quit now," Lessa said, grabbing a ski and slipping it back on.

"Lessa," he began.

"Go back up on the boat," she said, reaching for the other ski. "Please. I can do this."

He glanced back at the boat. Sabrina was leaning over the side, watching them. He could not argue with her here.

He hesitantly handed her the other ski and swam back to the boat. "She's determined," he said, pulling himself out of the water.

But he was about to learn just how tenacious she was. Time after time, Lessa went back down. Yet she showed no indication of being tired nor wishing to call it a day. She was hell-bent to succeed.

As Lessa took yet another tumble, Sabrina sighed and said, "How long will she keep his up?"

"Until she skis." He had no doubt that, if necessary, they would be at this all night.

"So, Rick," Sabrina said, leaning back against the

boat and stretching seductively, "you never did explain why you broke things off."

This was one conversation he had been hoping to avoid. "I thought we had an understanding," he said. "I wasn't ready for any commitment."

"And now you are?"

"I—" He hesitated, glancing in Lessa's direction. Her hair was a tangled mess but she didn't seem to care. She wiped her nose with the back of her arm and once again flashed the thumbs-up sign. He had to admit, there was something endearing in her refusal to give up. "I didn't plan on this happening with Lessa," he said quietly. "It was just one of those things."

He found himself encouraging Lessa silently from the sidelines. Her face set in grim determination, she slowly rose to her feet. Caught up in the moment, he jumped up and applauded. Lessa let out a whoop of joy.

Sabrina motioned to the driver to spin around. Rick knew that this would push Lessa outside of the wake, something which he thought was too dangerous. "No!" he shouted to Sabrina, but it was too late. Lessa sped outside the wake and in a split second, her slight form was lost in a spray of water.

He dove out of the boat, certain that no one could escape a fall like that unscathed. But once again, she surprised him.

"Did you see me?" she asked, bobbing in the water and grinning from ear to ear.

"You're lucky you didn't get hurt," he said gruffly, grabbing the skis.

"Lessa, I'm so sorry," Sabrina said, as they climbed

back onboard. "We were getting too far out, so I turned the boat...."

"You should've told her to drop the rope," Rick said angrily. No matter what Sabrina said, he knew better. It was intentional, and she was damn lucky that Lessa wasn't hurt. As it was, he thought, glancing at the big pink mark on Lessa's leg, she was going to have a hell of a bruise. "Do you have an ice pack?" he asked Sabrina.

"It's not necessary," Lessa said.

But Rick didn't listen. He helped her to sit down before holding the ice pack against her leg. "We've had enough. Let's head back."

Sabrina shrugged innocently and they drove back in silence. Rick's initial joy over Lessa's achievement faded into anger. What had she been trying to prove? It was stubbornness mixed with a sense of competition. She should've known when to throw in the towel, known when to say enough was enough. And as a result, she got hurt.

When they got back to shore, Rick made a point of keeping his arm around Lessa, helping her off the boat and down the dock.

"I'll see you at dinner," Sabrina said with a cheerful wave.

When they were out of earshot, Rick said, "What the hell were you doing back there—trying to kill yourself?"

"What are you talking about? I was waterskiing."

"You know very well what I'm talking about. You were trying to prove something. And your competitive nature almost got you seriously injured."

"I guess I should be touched that you're so concerned."

Why *was* he so annoyed? Maybe because the whole

scenario reminded him of what she had done at work. She had refused to give up, and as a result, she was about to get hurt. "You didn't have to prove anything, Lessa," he told her.

"I know that," she said, before shrugging off his arm. As she did so, her bathing-suit strap fell down over her pale, white shoulder. The wind gently blew the strands of her still-wet hair. Her eyes sparkled and her pale cheeks flushed with anger. He felt a sudden urge to kiss her.

"So how do you think it went with Sabrina?" she asked.

He forced himself to look away. The sight of her bare, slender body was enough to confuse even the most resolute intentions. "Hard to say."

"I think Sabrina is still interested in you."

"I told you that's over."

"Yeah, well, she had to look high and low to find a suit that skimpy."

"That's just how she dresses."

"And the way she kept touching you. Pretending to fall against you and putting on a show with the lotion."

"Jealous?" he teased.

"Me?" she asked. "Hardly. But I think Sabrina is."

But he knew better. Sabrina's flirtation was merely a test to see if he bit. He had no doubt that her line about her advisers reviewing the contract was just an excuse to stall for time. He and Lessa still had a lot of work to do if they were going to convince Sabrina. They needed to prove that their love was tempestuous and passionate. A love capable of desperate breakups and tearful reunions. "At dinner I'm going to ask Sabrina to dance. I want you to act like a jealous lover. I want you to storm out."

"Storm out? In other words, you want me to act like an idiot."

"No. I want you to act like a woman who believes her lover is flirting with another. I want you to act like a woman who cannot bear the thought of the man you love touching another woman."

"The man I love…" Her voice drifted off as the implication sank in. "Not all women behave so immaturely."

"True, but we are selling the whole firing as an act of passion. She needs proof. And she certainly didn't get it on the boat."

"Did it ever occur to you that the firing could've been your fault? Perhaps you quit because you saw me flirting with another man. And you couldn't stand the thought of me touching another."

"Sorry, sweetheart, but Sabrina knows me, remember?" he said, touching her cheek. His eyes hardened and he took her hand. "I'm not the jealous type."

Five

"So I'm not only immature enough to fire you over a love squabble, but I'm also jealous. What exactly do you see in me?"

What Rick saw was a woman with beautiful green eyes and exotic cheekbones. A woman with one of the most seductive bodies he had ever seen. A woman so stubborn and determined, she would suffer bruises and sprains without the slightest complaint until she learned how to water-ski. Instead, he said, "Perhaps you excel in other areas. Perhaps you're skilled—"

"In the bedroom? Is that what you were going to say?" She rolled her eyes and pulled her hand away.

"Actually, no. I was shooting for a good listener or cook, but I'd be more than happy with bedroom skills."

They walked back into the bungalow and shut the door. The air-conditioning was off and the room felt like an oven. She turned on the air conditioner and said, "This is going to be one long evening."

"Do you want to shower first or should I?"

"Go ahead," she said, sitting on top of the air-conditioner vent. "I'm set for a while."

Her long, slender legs were splayed out before her. The other bathing suit strap fell down. His eyes grazed down her neck and onto her bare shoulders. He swallowed and attempted to look in the other direction, then yanked off his shirt.

"You're not going to get undressed right here, are you?" she asked.

"No." In fact, he wasn't thinking about undressing himself, but her. What the hell was going on here? This was a business relationship. She was Alessandra Lawrence, the chairman of the board. The one who had fired him.

So why did he want to rip off her suit and take her right on the bed? Because Alessandra Lawrence just happened to be a beautiful woman. He always suspected as much, of course. But with her conservative suits and reserved manner, he'd never seen her as anything more than a wolf in sheep's clothing. He'd had her pegged as an uptight prude. He had not expected a spirited and feisty athlete. Nor had he ever expected her to look so good in a string bikini.

But there was something else that gave him pause. She had a quality, a way about her. There was a spark there. A connection. But whatever it was, it needed to be ignored. She was off-limits. Forever and always. This whole thing was make-believe. And he needed to keep it that way.

He let the freezing cold water of the shower pound

against him as he shut his eyes, trying not to notice his body's reaction to the woman just outside the door.

What had she gotten herself into? She was alone in a hotel room, ogling Rick Parker. She was—God help her—attracted to him. But how could she help it? They had spent the afternoon playing boyfriend and girlfriend. She had run her fingers over his raw muscles, felt the power of his kiss. And now here she was, only one closed door away from a naked Rick.

But, she attempted to reassure herself, it was normal, completely normal, that she feel some sort of attraction. After all, he was a good-looking man. Very good-looking. And she had a history with him. Like she had told Sabrina, she had suffered a painful crush.

But she couldn't allow herself to get confused. He was a business associate and that was all, one whom she did not even like. So why did a part of her wish that perhaps they were truly lovers? Why did a part of her wish that all their kissing and cuddling could lead to something else?

She would simply block it from her mind. She closed her eyes. *Just breathe,* she told herself. *And again…*

But she couldn't stop thinking about Rick. She remembered overhearing a conversation about him in the ladies' room a while ago. A woman in a neighboring stall had apparently known someone whom Rick had dated. Not realizing that Lessa was in the bathroom as well, the woman had said to her friend, "She said Rick told her on their first date that he didn't want any commitment."

"So what happened?" the other woman had asked.

"She slept with him anyway," the woman had said.

"Did he call her after that?"

"Nope. She was disappointed, of course. You know how it is. We all want to believe we're 'the one.' But she said it was worth it. She said he's great in bed."

"Great in bed?"

"Between you and me," the woman said, "I made a pass at him right after that."

"And?"

"He said no. He was very nice about it, but he said we work together. You know, he didn't want an office affair."

Great in bed...

Lessa turned up the air conditioner, as if a blast of cold air might cool her off. She had to stop thinking like this. Maybe if she had more of a social life, maybe if she *had* a social life, she wouldn't even notice Rick.

Unfortunately, it had been years since she'd been intimate with a man. And her last date had been months earlier, when her aunt had fixed her up with a friend's grandson. On paper he had sounded great, an engineer and part-time pro at a tennis club in the city. But it had been a disaster, right down to the three gold chains around his neck and the way he'd referred to every woman they'd encountered—the waitress, the hostess, the old lady whose cab he'd tried to steal—as "doll." The icing on the cake had been when he'd told her that for a businesswoman she had a "nice rack." And he should know, he'd added, because he'd "known"—big wink—a lot of businesswomen.

She knew her aunt blamed her long hours for her lack of a social life, but Lessa knew the problem was more complicated than that. After all, what twenty-six-year-old woman these days had only slept with one man?

One sexual affair to her credit and that had ended five years ago. Since then, she hadn't dated anyone longer than a week or two. And it wasn't just her love life that was suffering. Her entire social life was lacking. She had tried to make friends since she had come to New York to work for Lawrence, but it was difficult. Everyone she met was connected with Lawrence. Men were intimidated by her position and women tended to avoid her like the plague. One time she had invited a potential friend out for coffee only to find that the woman had not slept the night before, so worried was she that Lessa's invitation had been a ruse to fire her.

The truth of the matter was that Lessa didn't fit in with people her own age any more than she fit in with her fellow board members. Patience, her aunt had told her. It will all change with time.

But how could it when she spent all of her time at work? There was no way around it: She was lonely. It had gotten so bad that lately she had begun to wonder if perhaps she was destined for a life without love.

"It's freezing in here."

At the sound of Rick's voice, she turned. The sight of him, standing in the doorway with a mere towel around his waist, was enough to take her breath away. "You couldn't get dressed?" she asked, quickly averting her eyes.

"Not without my clothes."

She hurried past him and into the bathroom. He had left the shower running for her. She hurriedly took off her suit and stepped into the warm water. Only then did she realize that her clothes were still in the other room. She had been so flustered when Rick had come out in a towel that she had neglected to get her things. Now she had no choice but to do the same thing she had faulted Rick for—parade through the room in a towel. She finished her shower and grabbed the sole remaining towel, drying off and wrapping it tightly around her. Sabrina's decor might be nice but her towels left a lot to be desired. Thin and small, it barely covered Lessa's backside.

She opened the door and took a deep breath. What was the big deal? Rick had seen her in a bathing suit, and the towel covered more than that did. She glanced at her clothes on the chair and quickly calculated the amount of time she would be half-naked in front of Rick. To walk over and grab them, twenty seconds max. The key was to act as if she weren't embarrassed. To appear cool and in control.

Rick glanced up when the door opened. And there she was, wrapped only in a towel. For a split second he thought that perhaps she had come out to seduce him. But when she didn't look at him, when she walked right past him, he realized what had happened. She, like him, had forgotten her clothes. But if nothing else, he was a gentleman. He pulled a contract out of his briefcase and perused it, trying not to notice the way the towel slid open, revealing her leg. The way her plump white breasts peeked out of the top.

She hurried back inside the bathroom and when she came out again, she was dressed in her suit skirt and sleeveless blouse, holding her jacket in her hand.

She tossed her jacket on the bed and checked her watch. "Should we go?" Without waiting for him to answer, she walked outside.

"Lessa, wait," he said, tossing down the contract and following. "Aren't you forgetting something?"

She shook her head. "I don't think so."

"We're lovers, remember?" he said, sliding his arm around her waist. But the unhappiness in her eyes was almost enough to cool his desire. "It's almost over with," he said, as much to her as to himself. "As soon as she signs the papers we can go back to business as usual."

They walked down a winding path, following the signs to the restaurant. Although the sun had nearly set, it was still hot and muggy. They wove their way around thick patches of bougainvillea and tropical ferns, lit with multicolored spotlights. The restaurant was situated on a hill overlooking the sea. Completely open to the outside, it was lit only by candles, their flames flickering in the warm breeze. Rick gave the hostess their names and they were promptly led to a small, intimate table in the corner.

"I don't see her," Lessa said.

"I don't either," Rick said, taking the seat next to her. "But that doesn't mean she's not watching us."

"What should we do?"

"Let's just talk like two people who are interested in what the other has to say."

She glanced nervously at the door. She looked so uncomfortable he felt almost sorry for her. What had happened to the cool and collected woman from the office? The one who had fired him and then just as quickly negotiated his return?

"Where are you from?" she asked.

"I grew up outside the city. In fact, my parents still live in the same house."

"Do you have any brothers or sisters?"

"I have a sister and a brother."

"Do you see them often?"

"Fairly."

This was painful. She was looking everywhere but at him. "So, Lessa," he said, touching her hand to get her attention, "what are your plans for Christmas?"

"My Gran and I are going to have a quiet dinner. Just the two of us."

"Your grandmother?"

"No. She's my great-aunt. My only family. She fell down a year ago and hurt her hip, so I moved her in with me. She's better now but I like having her around."

She lived with her aunt? The image of Alessandra as a sweet and caring niece did not jive with the cold, self-reliant woman he knew from the office. "That's nice of you to take care of her."

"It's the least I could do. After all, she took me in after my dad died. She'd never had any children and she took the role of surrogate parent very seriously. She was great about the whole tennis thing. Even though she was already older she flew with me all over the world. She attended every match."

"I heard you turned down an opportunity to go pro."

"I don't know about that," she said modestly. "But I knew that if I chose to go any further, it would've taken all my energy and time. I wouldn't have been able to go to school or get my MBA."

"Education is important, but not many people turn down an opportunity to be a professional athlete."

"Ultimately I felt like I had little choice. I made a promise to my father."

"You promised him you'd get your degree?"

"No," she said, her eyes meeting his. "I promised him I'd get his company back. I knew in order to do that, I was going to need all the education and experience I could get."

He sat there for a moment, too stunned to speak. He had always known that she was on some sort of mission to take over the company, but he had never imagined that it was an instruction that had come from Howard Lawrence himself.

"But I still play tennis," she said. "At least, as much as I can. I've even fantasized about investing in a tennis camp one day. Either on my own or through Lawrence…and now we're back on business." She grinned apologetically and shrugged. "I'm not very good at this small talk, am I?" Without giving him a chance to answer, she asked, "What are you doing for Christmas?"

"I'm sure I'll be working," he said. He wanted to question Lessa more about her promise to her father, but now was not the time. Not with Sabrina lurking about. He had to take advantage of Lessa's question to steer the conversation back to neutral ground.

"At the office?"

"No. I usually visit one of the resorts, " he said.

"Not exactly Norman Rockwell."

"Norman Rockwell?"

"The big family sitting around the table while the father carves the turkey. My aunt is always apologizing for my lack of family. She blames herself for not having children. She'd like nothing better than the big family gathering, crammed with kids and noise."

"Well, if noise is what you're looking for, you'd love

my family get-togethers. Deafening." He smiled and said, "My brother and sister aren't too bad, but I have a big extended family. Lots of cousins, nieces and nephews. Family dinners are pretty crazy. "

"Your brother and sister are married?"

"They've both been married and divorced. In fact, my sister is about to get married again."

She took a sip of her wine. "So you're the only one who has never been married?"

"Or divorced, as the case may be. I'm the anomaly. They can't quite figure me out. So every time we all get together the big discussion is usually about who they are going to fix me up with."

"But you hardly need help finding dates."

"Apparently they don't like my choices."

"You've brought a lot of girlfriends home?"

"I've only made that mistake a couple of times." He shook his head. "Disasters. But then again, they all loved Karen." All these years later, it was still difficult to talk about her.

"Karen?"

"I was engaged a long time ago."

Conversation died and the room seemed to go quiet. So much for neutral ground. Why had he mentioned Karen? He never spoke of her. Most people at the office had no idea he'd ever been engaged.

"And what happened? No, let me guess. You stood her up at the altar in front of three hundred guests."

"No. *Let it go,* he warned himself. *Switch the subject.* But for some reason, he couldn't. It was the way she was looking at him, so certain that her impression of him as a cold, uncaring bastard was correct. "She died."

She sat still, stunned.

"I was still in grad school. I was studying, so I asked her to come to my apartment after work. She was half a block away when a drunk driver hit her. I don't think I'll ever forget that moment. To pick up the phone and hear a stranger tell me that she wasn't coming home…that she was never coming home."

"I'm so sorry."

He expected her to glance away, to do what most people did when they found out. To make some off-the-cuff comment and attempt to change the subject, but she didn't. She looked straight at him and said, "I can't imagine anything more awful. You must miss her."

"We were high-school sweethearts. We dated all through college. I thought I had everything planned out. We were going to buy a house, have kids. And in a split second, it was all gone." He ran his fingers through his hair. Why was he telling her this?

"My father suffered the same kind of loss," she said. "My mother got sick and died only a month later. They had been high-school sweethearts, too. He never got over it either."

He had known that Howard's wife had died and he had known that she had been his original partner. But he had never thought about the implications of that partnership.

"You know, when my father died, my Gran said he was still right here," she said, putting her hand over her heart. "And that part of him would never die, it would always be right there. And she was right. I can still feel him."

He could see the pain in her eyes and was struck by an urge to soothe her. "How old were you when your mother died?" he asked.

"I was three. I don't really remember much about her. My dad never really spoke of her but my Gran said she was one of the most determined and feisty people you'd ever want to meet. She said that from the first moment my father met her, he fell in love. My aunt said he was devastated when she died. He shut down. He dated, but he never saw the same woman longer than a month. I think he just couldn't stand any more pain. He couldn't allow anyone in because he was afraid of getting hurt again."

Rick glanced away. Without realizing it, she had just summarized his life. "Or maybe," he said, "he never again met anyone that special."

"Maybe," she said. "I'd like to think my parents shared the kind of love that comes along once in a lifetime."

"I'm sure they did," he said.

Her eyes, misty with emotion, narrowed. "I know what you think about me, Rick. The spoiled woman motivated by greed. I know you think I have no right to this company. But you have no idea how important this business was to my dad. It was more than a job, much more. He and my mother started it together and he felt that this company was *still* an extension of her somehow. That he was fulfilling her dream. Their life together."

"Lessa," he began. But what could he say? She was right. He did think that she was a spoiled girl with a keen sense of entitlement. And although she was turning out to be more complicated than he had thought, he could not—no, he *would not*—allow emotion to cloud his judgment.

But before he could say anything, she spoke. "Sabrina's behind you."

He put his arm around Lessa and slipped his hand under her shirt, caressing her bare shoulder. "Act as though I just said something very sweet," he whispered.

She smiled at him, but it was obvious that his touch made her uncomfortable. Apparently their conversation had done little to change her feelings toward him. If she wasn't careful, Sabrina would be on to them.

He felt a presence behind him and heard Sabrina say, "Well, what do you think of my dining room? It truly is romantic, isn't it?" She walked around the table and took a seat across from him.

"Did you bring the contract?" he asked.

She shook her head. "My adviser is looking it over. He should have it to me momentarily. So you might as well enjoy your dinner," she said, signaling a waiter.

Lessa ordered a steak and a side of rice.

"I'll have the same," Rick said. He appreciated a woman who was willing and able to eat.

"How compatible," Sabrina said. "You even order the same food." But it was obvious from the tone in her voice, she thought them anything but. They were going to have to lay it on thick to convince her.

"So do you two live together?"

"I live with my aunt," Lessa said.

"Your aunt? How sweet. And what does she think of your romance with Rick?"

"She's pleased with…our relationship," Lessa said, hesitating.

"Really? After what Rick did to your father?"

He could feel Lessa stiffen.

"I don't know what you're talking about," she said.

"Rick didn't have anything to do with my father leaving the company."

Unfortunately, it was obvious her defense of him was an act. He could practically see the strain on her face.

"Besides, my aunt wants me to be happy," she said with some effort. "She knows that I didn't plan this. But she respects my decision."

"Isn't that wonderful?" Sabrina said, studying Lessa carefully. Sabrina was suspicious and things were getting worse by the minute. He needed to get Lessa away from her. Just then the band began to play.

"Darling," he said, standing and offering Lessa his hand, "it's our song." He turned back toward Sabrina. "Will you excuse us?"

"Of course," she said with a smug smile.

He led Lessa to the dance floor. He pulled her in close as he whispered in her ear, "I think I need to kiss you again."

If Sabrina wanted a show, she was going to get it. He brushed a gentle kiss across Lessa's porcelain cheek. She turned toward him and their lips touched. A sensuous tremor passed between them as he pulled her tight against him. Momentarily forgetting about his mission, he kissed her long and hard, as if she were a true lover. Suddenly, Lessa broke away. Her breasts heaved as she struggled to breathe. She glanced at Rick and he knew from the look in her eyes that they were in trouble.

"Lessa," he said, leaning forward and touching the back of his hand to her cheek. "Are you all right?"

"I'm sorry," she whispered. Before he could stop her, she turned and hurried toward the door.

Damn her! What was she doing? He went after her,

following her outside the restaurant. He grabbed her arm and spun her around to face him. "Just what in the hell do you think you're doing?"

"I can't do this," she said, shrugging off his arm. The look on her face gave him pause. She didn't look like a woman in control of her feelings and actions. She was shaking and appeared to be on the verge of tears.

He hesitated and, without touching her, nodded toward the beach. "Let's get away from the restaurant." He had no doubt Sabrina was bending over backward to get a peek of the action. "Let me guess," he said as they walked toward the beach. "There's a boyfriend back home and you're feeling guilty."

"No. There's no boyfriend."

He felt a small gleam of relief. But why should he care if she was seeing someone?

"I'm just...unsure of the ground rules."

"The ground rules?" What the hell was she talking about? Did she interpret his touch as true longing?

But if she did, would she be wrong? After all, there was an undercurrent of...something. "Look, Lessa," he said, "this isn't one of your tennis matches. There are no rules or regulations. When Sabrina's around, I touch you, you touch me. That's all."

He saw her wince as if in pain. Was the mere idea of touching him so repulsive to her?

"Just pretend I'm...someone else. Someone you care about. Someone you saw in a movie once, hell, I don't care. Forget about my face and just respond to my actions. That's all."

"I'm trying, but it's difficult."

"Dammit," he said, getting even more frustrated.

"Let me make this clear. I'm not enjoying myself either. But this is business. You almost cost me my company and you better try damn hard to get it back."

She did not speak. She looked at him with all the fear and loathing to which he had become accustomed. But for some reason, it wasn't okay anymore. He felt like a bully.

He should've realized that this was too much to ask of her. After all, she hated him. How could he think that she was capable of pretending otherwise? "I should've known that you couldn't do this." He turned away, heading back toward the restaurant. "Go back to the room and wait for me. I'll handle Sabrina."

Rick's words hit Lessa like a splash of ice water. Couldn't do this? Was she really ready to forfeit simply because she didn't like the way the game was being played? Because that was what their whole fake love affair boiled down to—a strategy. The problem was, she couldn't help but wish it were real. With a kiss and some kind emotional words, Rick slashed through the paper-thin barrier surrounding her heart. The promise of love was enough to make her question even the most fundamental of views. But she had to get over it.

She hurried after Rick and took his hand, stopping him. Then, gazing into his eyes, she stood on her tip-toes and pressed her lips to his. She moved her mouth over his, allowing her instincts to take over. She kissed him long and slow, as if he were the man of her dreams and this was the chance of a lifetime. When she was done, she pulled away and said, "Better?"

He was breathing hard and his eyes smoldered with fire. "I'd say."

She smiled, pleased at his reaction. "I can do this. Let's go."

They walked back into the dining room. Their dinner had arrived but Sabrina was nowhere to be seen. He led her back to the table and gulped down his entire glass of champagne, then poured himself another.

"Careful, dear," she said, leaning forward just enough for him to get a peek at her cleavage. "You know how you get when you drink."

She saw his gaze wander down to her breasts before gulping down some more champagne.

"There's Sabrina," she said. As she watched Sabrina work the crowd, flashing various diners a fake, almost frightening smile, Lessa tried to imagine the woman arm in arm with Rick. "I don't see you with her," she said in between bites.

He glanced at Sabrina and said, "I think she was different then. She wasn't as...hard as she is now."

"Hmm. That's probably what my old boyfriends say about me."

"Oh? There are a lot of them?"

She'd meant it as a joke, but he seemed to take her seriously. "No. Not really."

"And why is that?"

"Because..." Why was she suddenly feeling as if she were in a therapy session? Was he going to pay the kindly uncle and give her dating tips? "I've been busy."

"An excuse. But not bad. I've used it myself."

"But you date. You date a lot. It seems like every time I turn around there's another mention of you with a different woman."

"You've been working with me now for six months. Is that your impression of me?"

No, at least not in the office. She would give him that. But there was a question she was dying to ask. "Are you involved with anyone right now?"

"No."

A surge of relief flooded her veins. But why should she care? She waited for him to finish his meal and then said, "Let's dance."

She took his hand and led him out to the dance floor. She wrapped her arms tightly around his neck. She could not only act like a lover, she could act like a temptress. And she was just getting warmed up. "Aren't you going to hold me?" she said softly.

"What got into you?"

"I don't like to give up a game."

"Ah, I see. Everything changed when I told you to go back to the room. You took it as a dare."

"I took it as intended. A challenge."

"And Alessandra Lawrence does not back away from a challenge."

"I know that you have me pegged as a spoiled rich girl, but that couldn't be further from the truth. I'm very determined and I'm willing to work hard to get what I want."

"I believe that, Lessa." He gazed at her, as if drinking her in. "So who am I tonight?" he asked. "Are you pretending I'm a famous movie star...or a—"

"Andre Agassi." The truth of the matter was that there was no need to pretend he was anyone other than himself. But she could not admit that to him.

"A tennis player, of course. I should've guessed." He

smiled. "You're not what I expected, Lessa. I never thought that I would enjoy spending time with you."

Her heart jumped into her throat. He was enjoying her company? "Is this part of your plan to convince Sabrina?" she joked. "You sweet talk me and I fall madly in love with you?"

"Do you think that would work?" he asked, flashing her his famous grin.

He was teasing and she knew it, yet she couldn't stop herself from answering. "If that's your plan," she said, playing along, "I should warn you it might be more difficult than you think. I've never been in love before."

"That's too bad," he said.

"I'm not so sure," she replied. "I've seen the havoc it wreaked on some of my friends."

"Not all love affairs end badly," he said. "And even those that do…well, sometimes it's still worth it."

His eyes grew distant and she knew he was thinking about the woman he had loved all those years before. She was possessed by a sudden urge to comfort him. "I'm sorry," she said quietly.

He did not speak but cupped her chin tenderly.

She closed her eyes, reveling in the touch. His arm slid around her as he pulled her closer. The act caught her off guard, taking away her breath. He leaned forward to kiss her, and her senses charged to life as a delicious shudder rippled through her body. He softly touched his lips to hers.

"There you are!" Sabrina said, interrupting. "I was wondering if I might be able to steal him away for a moment." Looking at Rick, she said, "You promised me a dance."

To Lessa, it almost looked as if he regretted leaving her. She stepped aside and Rick swept Sabrina into his arms. As Sabrina wrapped her arms around his neck and nestled her cheek against his, Lessa felt jealous. Real, honest-to-goodness jealous.

What was happening here? She wasn't supposed to feel jealous. She wasn't supposed to feel anything at all. It was all an act. He was Rick Parker, her nemesis, the man who'd stolen her father's company. There was no possibility of anything happening between them, ever.

But she couldn't help wishing things might be different. She couldn't help her body from enjoying his kisses and hoping for more.

Sabrina put her arms around Rick's neck. Lessa was once again the girl in the doorway, lusting after a man who did not even know she existed.

If she was going to storm out in a fit of jealousy, now would be the time. With one last glance, she made her way toward the door. Just as she got to it, she felt a hand on her arm. Rick spun her around and, pulling her close, kissed her once again.

Six

It was the velvet kiss Lessa had dreamed of, the one she had longed for all those years ago. She wrapped her arms around Rick's neck, welcoming him. His arm slid around her as he pulled her closer. Her senses charged to life. It was as if time had stopped. Nothing else mattered. She wanted to feel him, all of him.

And then, just as suddenly as it had all started, it stopped. "Let's get out of here," he said, breaking away.

His words suggested an intimacy, a desire to be alone. But she knew better. She could tell by the look in his eyes that something was wrong. "But the contract..."

"She's not signing the contract tonight. It was all a game."

Accepting his hand, Lessa followed him out the door. Once outside, he stepped away from her.

"What did she say?" she asked as he led her down to

the beach. It was a warm tropical night. The sky was littered with stars and a heavy, full moon that reflected off the glittering sea.

"She's put us off until morning." He stopped and let go of her hand. "I think she's playing with us, Lessa. I don't think she bought our story, unless our last-ditch effort convinced her. I don't think she has any intention of signing that contract tomorrow."

"I'm sorry. I'm afraid I wasn't very convincing as the jealous girlfriend."

"You did fine." He smiled at her again. It was genuine and sincere, not like the patronizing grins to which she had grown accustomed.

"What are you suggesting we do?" she asked.

"We can go back to New York and try to come up with another way to fend off this takeover. Or," he said, after hesitating, "we can give it another night."

Another night. A night sharing the same room. She glanced toward the water slowly licking the shore. "I didn't bring a change of clothes, or anything," she said.

"I know how you feel about this, Lessa," he said. "So if you want to go home tonight, I understand. I'll stay and deal with Sabrina alone tomorrow morning."

As she followed him back toward their bungalow. She felt the jealous whisper of uneasiness. She thought back to the way Sabrina had leaned into him, the way she had looked at him. Did he want Lessa to leave so that he could have a secret rendezvous with the enemy? Perhaps he had decided on a different way to convince Sabrina to abort the takeover. "She propositioned you, didn't she?"

"How did you know that?" he replied in a tone that let her know her hunch was correct.

The thought of Sabrina propositioning the man Lessa was supposed to be with was infuriating, to say the least. The thought of him accepting was even more infuriating. "What did you say?" she asked, her voice cold.

"I don't mix business and pleasure, Lessa," he said, stopping in front of their bungalow.

"Not even with an old girlfriend?"

He unlocked their door and pushed it open. When she walked inside, he stepped in front of her. "Not even with an old girlfriend," he said, his voice low and threatening. "Now make up your mind. Are you staying or not?"

She looked at the solitary bed. She could've sworn the room was even smaller than when they'd left it. "I'm staying," she said.

He paused for a moment and then stepped away. He loosened his tie and closed the blinds. It was obvious he was angry with her for suggesting that perhaps he would have a liaison with Sabrina. But how could she not suspect the worst? After all, the image of him dancing with Sabrina was burned in her mind. The way he had held her in his arms. The way he had looked at her.

Lessa walked over to the bed and sat on the edge. "Did you love her?"

"Love her?" he asked, surprised. "No. I told you, we had a brief affair. I don't think it lasted more than a week. That was all." He sat down next to her and said, "You're going to have to trust me on this one, Lessa."

"I'm sorry, Rick. Regardless of what you say, I don't think I can ever trust you. Actions are stronger than words."

"I assume the action in my case is what happened to your father. And that doesn't define me as anything but a businessman. I was given an offer and I took it. I did what I could to help him. I'm the one who put together his severance package. I'm the reason you inherited your stock."

"Do you think I should thank you? Losing this company destroyed him." It had literally broken his heart. He had suffered a fatal heart attack and died less than a month later.

"Lessa," he said softly. "He was a good man who did a great job building this company—but he is the one who took it public and hired the board. And you know as well as I do that whenever you take a company public you lose some control."

"He fought so hard to keep his job. I hardly saw him during that last year."

"I'm sorry, Lessa," Rick said quietly. "It's not all about hard work. Sometimes people are simply outmatched."

Was he talking about her father or her? "I realize that. But if you're referring to me, I conceded, remember? And now we're partners on the same team."

He glanced away. Whatever may have transpired between them, it was obvious he still harbored doubt about her.

"I need to have your support, Rick," she said.

His eyes softened and he smiled slightly. He glanced at her leg. "How is it feeling?" he asked, running his finger around the bruise.

"Great," she said, her response indicating not the pain from her bruise but the exquisite feel of his touch. Their eyes locked and she could feel her heart turn over. Her entire body ached for him. He leaned forward and she closed her eyes, readying for his kiss.

* * *

In the nick of time, Rick stopped. What the hell was he doing?

He needed to get back to business. The night, the wine, the romantic setting…it was all making him lose his head. She was not a lover he had brought on vacation, nor would she ever be. She was the chairman of the board and he couldn't allow himself to forget it.

He grabbed his laptop and sat in the chair, trying not to notice as she settled herself on the bed. She fluffed up the pillows before situating her computer on her lap. If anyone had looked in the window, he would think they were a happily settled domestic couple, albeit one not romantically inclined.

He sorted through the day's mail and messages before scouring the recent stock activity. "Sabrina has been buying more stock," he said.

He picked up his laptop and took it over to the bed to show her. He sat beside her and said, "Look at this."

She scanned the information. "So she has no intention of selling her shares to us?"

"Not necessarily. She might be doing this just because she knows we want it. She figures whatever she has is worth twice as much."

"Maybe we should draft a letter to the stockholders and tell them what's going on. They need to know that now is not the time to sell."

"I agree," Rick said.

Together they began to work. At close to two in the morning, Lessa fell asleep, her head on Rick's shoulder. A copper ringlet had fallen over her forehead. He gazed across her face, slowly lingering on her temptingly curved mouth. He slid his hand under her head and gently set her down on the pillow. She sighed and the corners of her lips turned upwards in a sweet smile as she nestled into the soft down.

Damn, but he wanted her.

He swallowed hard and, utilizing every ounce of willpower he could summon, rolled out of bed. Her rubbing up against him in the middle of the night could trigger a chain of events that he didn't want to think about.

He settled himself into the chair and leaned backward, absentmindedly running his fingers through his hair. Who would've thought he'd want to make love to Alessandra Lawrence? She had been nothing but trouble. He'd found her uptight and rigid, a prim and proper woman with a narrow vision. And, so he thought, they had nothing in common besides their desire to run Lawrence Enterprises.

But beneath that cool exterior was a warm and passionate woman, one with her own struggles and demons. And one who just happened to look damn good in a towel.

He barely slept that night. He tossed and turned until a sliver of light was shining through the rose-colored curtains. As he massaged his stiff neck, Lessa sighed slightly and turned on her back. Her long eyelashes curled over her sleeping eyes, and her hair was splayed out behind her. Her body, long and elegant, rested on top of the covers. Daylight had not helped his willpower. With the light radiating around her, she looked like an angel. At the very least, she was the most beautiful woman he had ever seen.

He needed to get out of there. Fast. He showered and

dressed as quickly as he could. When he walked back in the room, Lessa was sitting on the side of the bed.

"Good morning," she said, stretching like a lazy kitten. Her hair was tousled and her shirt half-unbuttoned. And the fact that she was unaware of her sexiness only added to her allure.

"I'm going to find some coffee," he said, looking away. "How do you take it?"

"Black, please," she said as he shut the door.

He picked up the coffee in the restaurant and took his time getting back to the bungalow. He paused outside the door and saw Sabrina stepping off a boat, dressed all in white. She was a beautiful woman, but she paled in comparison to Lessa. He found it amazing that he had ever been attracted to her. She seemed so superficial and insincere. But he had not been looking for love when they'd gotten together. He had been looking for sex and adventure and had found her significantly lacking in both.

He could not imagine coming home to a woman like that. He wanted a woman more like Lessa, one who was spunky and tough. A woman who could be sensitive and strong at the same time. Sabrina saw him and waved. He nodded in her direction and pushed open the door.

Lessa was standing with her back to him, wearing only a pair of lace panties. She pulled her dress over her head and spun around.

"Don't you knock?" she said, picking up her bra and heading back into the bathroom.

"Look, Lessa, I'm sorry. Sabrina is right outside the door. It never occurred to me that you would be naked in the middle of the room. After all, the blinds aren't even closed."

The bathroom door opened and she reappeared. "It's all right," she said. "No harm done."

He would beg to differ. He had seen her full, ripe breasts, her tiny flat belly and the panties that hung over her slender hips. It was a sight he was not going to forget anytime soon.

He suddenly realized that he hadn't moved. He was still standing in the doorway, holding the coffee in front of him.

"Is this mine?" she asked, taking a cup. He watched her sip the warm liquid. She sighed and closed her eyes. "Mmm. This tastes great," she said, running her tongue around her lips. "Thank you."

What was she trying to do, drive him crazy?

Oblivious to her charm, she smiled and said, "Now I'm ready for another round." She opened the door and waved to Sabrina. Then she turned back toward him and whispered, "We should kiss."

Without hesitation, she stood on her tiptoes and wrapped her arms around his neck. As her lips touched his, he could feel his body respond.

Unaware of the seductive spell she had cast, she pulled away. "Did she see?" she asked cheerfully.

"I'd say so." Sabrina was walking straight toward them. "Good morning, Sabrina," he said as Lessa turned around.

"How did you sleep?" Sabrina asked.

"Did we sleep?" Lessa teased with an obvious wink.

"No," he answered truthfully. "I didn't sleep at all."

Ignoring the fact that Lessa was practically glued to him, Sabrina touched his cheek. "Tsk, tsk. And the mattresses are guaranteed to provide a good night's sleep."

"Oh, we did enjoy the mattress," Lessa said, rubbing her hand against Rick's chest.

"Are you ready to sign?" he asked Sabrina. Any more talk like this and he was going to have to toss Lessa back onto the bed and test out the mattress himself.

Sabrina sighed dramatically. "I'm afraid we're going to have to postpone once again. It seems my research has not been thorough."

"How unfortunate," Lessa said.

"I'm going to need a few more days," Sabrina said with a shrug. "It was nice meeting you, Lessa. I certainly do hope you enjoyed your stay. Rick," she said, pausing to flash him a stiff smile, "I'll be in touch." She spun on her heels and turned away, walking quickly back toward the office.

"You were right. She had no intention of signing that contract," Lessa said when Sabrina was out of earshot. She let go of Rick's arm and stepped away from him. "This whole strategy was a bust. It won't be difficult for her to find out that we're not together. After all, everyone at the office knows how we feel about each other."

"Perhaps we can change that."

"I don't know," she said. "Pretending we're together for a stranger is one thing, but doing this on a day-to-day basis?"

"We'll give them just enough to assume."

"What do you mean?"

"The office Christmas party is in a couple days," he said. "We'll go together. It should be enough to get the rumors going."

After all, everyone knew that he and Lessa had fought tooth and nail over the party. He had never liked

Christmas parties. Too much alcohol and partying had turned an otherwise diligent worker into the murderer who was responsible for Karen's death. But that was not the only reason he disliked office Christmas parties. They were a complete waste of time and money. It was a momentary pleasure at best, an obligatory occasion in an otherwise busy season at worst. But Lessa had insisted. The annual Christmas party had been a Howard Lawrence tradition.

"Right," she said, after a moment's hesitation. "I just hope it'll be enough."

"We'll get this company back one way or another," he said reassuringly. And then, before he could stop himself, he gave her hand an encouraging squeeze even though no one was there to see it.

Seven

Lessa knew from playing doubles that if a partnership was not strong there was little hope of winning the match. And so she had returned from the Bahamas with a fine-tuned strategy. There was only one way to win Rick's respect. She needed to prove she was a worthy partner.

Fortunately, she had found a way. She had studied the financials and had come to the conclusion that in order to increase the value of the stock, they needed to sell off some of their more expensive assets. That money could then be used to expand, to buy and develop other properties.

Like the property she had found in Florida. Located off the Gulf of Mexico, Mara del Ray was a former luxury resort, a diamond in the rough. Lessa had attended a tennis tournament there as a teenager and from the moment she'd heard that it was for sale she knew it would be perfect for Lawrence. But where would she get the money to buy it?

Fortunately, there was one resort in particular that was ripe to sell. Located in Antigua, it was now one of their most profitable. But that was certain to change. There was another major resort opening on the island and the resulting competition was bound to affect its value. Better to sell while they were on top. She had made some inquiries and was close to finding a buyer. When she found one, she hoped to present the whole package to Rick and prove once and for all that she knew what she was doing.

"But do you care what Rick thinks?" her aunt asked when Lessa shared the details of her plan.

Yes, she did. So much that when he had walked in and seen her naked, she had done her best to act as if it weren't a big deal. Even though she was mortified, she was not about to act like the hysterical woman who had run out on him the night before. And so she had swallowed her pride and pretended that showing her half-naked body to Rick Parker was something she did every day.

She told none of that to her great-aunt. All she said was "He's my partner, Gran. We have to get along."

"What exactly happened in the Bahamas?" her aunt asked suspiciously.

"Not much. We had a terrible meeting with Sabrina, and then…" Then they had gone back to the hotel room they'd shared. She'd put on a string bikini. They'd kissed, gone waterskiing, kissed again, gone dancing, kissed yet again and then she'd fallen asleep in his arms. Oh, and then, just in case he hadn't gotten a good enough look at her in the string bikini, she'd shown him what she looked like topless. "That was about it."

How could she give her elderly aunt the whole truth and nothing but the truth? She didn't want to upset her. And Lessa had no doubt Gran would be upset to learn that since returning from the Bahamas, her niece had been unable to forget about those damned kisses. They were enough to make her forget who she was and where she was going. But it was more than just a few kisses. It was the way he made her feel, as if she were the most interesting person in the world. More than interesting. He made her feel beautiful.

Her aunt was looking at her curiously, as if attempting to decipher the secret meaning behind her words. Lessa knew the woman was hot on her tracks and, in order to throw her off, she had to toss her a bone. "I must admit that Rick surprised me. He can be very charming when he wants." It was a gift, actually. He was blessed with the gift of sexual magnetism. She could still remember the way the assistants used to flutter around him at her father's office. The giggles and the seductive glimmer in their eyes when they referred to him.

Time, she thought. She just needed some time to clear her head before seeing him again.

"What do you mean?" her aunt asked.

"He was kind and considerate. He was actually worried about me when I was waterskiing."

"He sounds human. That doesn't make him kind."

"Did you know he was engaged? She died in a car accident. From the way he spoke about her, he still hasn't recovered. I think that's the reason he never married. He's still nursing a broken heart."

"Be careful, Lessa. A man like that, one who's been

so wounded, is not the best choice. It'll take quite a bit to heal his broken heart."

"I'm not going to heal his heart."

"But you would like to."

A heavy silence filled the room. Was her aunt right? Did she want to heal his heart?

It was true that she couldn't forget the feel of his hand on hers, the way she had felt when he had looked into her eyes and whispered her name. But it was ridiculous, the whole thing. A romantic fantasy inspired by a romantic setting. That was all.

"Of course not," Lessa finally responded. "If I feel anything, it's a crush. It's not real."

"I can't say I'm surprised you have a crush on him. It's the first time you've been alone with a man in how long?"

"I've been busy," she said defensively.

"Yes, yes, I know. You've been working. As I've told you before, a company can't take you out to dinner. They can't bring you soup when you're sick. They can't keep you warm on cold winter nights."

"I get it."

"A company can keep you busy, but it can't prevent loneliness. I'd like to think that if I'm not here next Christmas you'll have someone else beside you."

"Don't talk like that. You'll be here. As for my love life, who knows? I must admit, I'm a little more hopeful than I have been."

"Lessa," her aunt said, "a man like Rick may serve as a distraction, but that's all. A relationship with him is a complication you don't need."

"Don't worry, Gran. I'm not interested in having a relationship with Rick Parker."

She had told her aunt a partial truth. She may not want a relationship with him, but one thing was certain. She was dying to kiss him again.

By the time Lessa left work, it was close to seven o'clock. The air was crisp and it felt as if it might snow. She paused to wrap her scarf around her neck as she glanced at the store window display. It was a scene right out of a Christmas fairy tale. Snow was falling as a couple kissed underneath trees lined with mistletoe. Just as she started feeling sentimental about the special holiday approaching, a pellet of freezing rain hit her on the nose. She glanced at the cloud-covered sky. The rain was a reminder that in real life, mistletoe trees did not exist and it didn't always snow on Christmas. And sometimes, as much as she and her aunt might wish otherwise, there was no one to kiss under the mistletoe.

She turned away from the window and hurried to the street corner. From the crowd of people desperately trying to hail a cab, she knew her chances of getting one were slim to none. And raining or not, she had promised her aunt a Christmas tree. She would just have to hoof it to the tree vendor as fast as she could. As the horns blew and the people pushed and shoved, her thoughts once again drifted back to palm trees, warm, quiet nights and the man she had kissed.

She had to snap out of this. It was one thing to please a business partner, quite another to dream about seducing him. Although she had spent the day putting together her Antigua deal, pesky thoughts kept interrupting her noble motives. Like how damn good he looked in swim trunks and the expression on his face when he'd opened the door and seen her half-naked.

In fact, several times that day, she had found herself at the water fountain outside his office, unable to quench her thirst. She was as bad as a teenager with a crush. But she had to forget about what happened in the Bahamas. She was not a kid anymore; she was the chairman of the board and Rick was her partner.

A partner whom she had barely seen since their return. In spite of his desire to cultivate the pretense of a romance, the most contact they had had was an occasional hello in the hallway. There were no meaningful glances, no secret rendezvous, no—

"Lessa?"

She turned around. Rick was behind her, looking every bit the dapper executive. He was wearing a black cashmere coat with a maroon scarf tucked inside. "Hi," she managed to say.

"Here," he said, opening his umbrella. "Stand under this."

"No thanks. Contrary to rumors, I won't melt."

"I insist." He smiled as he stepped closer, sheltering her from the rain. "Which way are you going?"

"Fifty-eighth and First," thinking of the Christmas tree lot.

"My car is parked in a lot near here. I'll drive you." Her heart jumped into her throat at the thought of being alone with him. They walked to the next corner in silence.

As they waited for the light to change, she could feel him looking at her. Suddenly self-conscious, she smoothed her damp hair and dabbed at the mascara she was certain had smeared under her eye. "I must look like a drowned rat," she said.

"You look beautiful," he said softly.

Beautiful. He said *beautiful.*

Suddenly she was aware of him, very aware. His masculine presence seemed to fill the night. She felt a chill run down her spine and wrapped her arms around her damp trench coat. In her rush to get out of the house that morning, she had taken a coat that was better suited to a warm spring day than a blustery winter night.

"Hold this," he said, handing her the umbrella. He shrugged off his overcoat and gave it to her. "Put this on."

"No, that's all right. I'm fine."

"I insist."

"But then you'll be cold."

"Put it on," he said again. After she hesitated, he added, "I think you know that I'm every bit as stubborn as you."

Once again she found herself obeying. She wrapped his coat around her, reveling in its musky scent.

"How have things been going for you at the office? Have you been having an easier time?" he asked as they walked down Fifth Avenue. Little gold lights sparkled on the barren trees, and store windows beckoned with spectacular holiday displays.

"No one's poisoned my coffee but they're not exactly standing in line to shake my hand either. I did overhear some women discussing me in the bathroom however. Seems that word of our overnight in the Bahamas is making the gossip circuit. Quite frankly, I think some of the women in the office are hoping that we *are* having a romance. That maybe our office romance will pave the way for more."

"What do you mean, pave the way?"

"Come on now," she teased. "You've noticed how the women there flock around you."

He shook his head and squinted his eyes. "What are you talking about?"

"Rick, you must know that many women who work with you harbor a secret, and sometimes not-so-secret, crush. They know you have a rule about avoiding office romances. They figure you getting involved with me can only be good. After all, if you broke your rule with me, then maybe you'll break it with them as well." There. She had spelled it out.

"So they're assuming we're going to break up?"

"I think it's safe to say the answer is a big yes. After all, you're not exactly a one-woman man."

"I see," he said with a twinkle in his eye. He was obviously enjoying this conversation. "I'll tell you what. When it comes time to break up, I'll let you do the honors."

"That would be quite a claim to fame. I fire you *and* break up with you. I'll go down in history."

He laughed, a deep and hearty response. She couldn't help but feel proud to have elicited such a reaction. His laughs were few and far between. He hesitated and the look in his eyes softened. "Well then, we'll have to give them something to talk about tomorrow night."

As she looked into his eyes, her heart jumped. Tomorrow night was the Christmas party, an event she had worked hard to produce. Up until now, she had viewed it with anxiety, yet another project for which she would be held accountable. But the thought of attending it with Rick, the thought of having to pretend once again that they were lovers, was enough to elicit a tingle of excitement. She cleared her throat, pretending not to be affected. "That's right," she said.

She glanced beside her, suddenly realizing that they were in front of Saks department store. Every Christmas, Saks decorated their windows with magnificent Christmas displays. This year's were the most amazing yet. Each window contained a mannequin dressed in haute couture, posed in fabulous scenes meant to represent a fantasy.

The window directly in front of them contained a mannequin dressed like a woman from the eighteen-hundreds. She looked elegant and wealthy in her diamond tiara and jewelry. But she sat in a slump in an expensive chair, her beautiful gown flouncing around her gold slippers. In her hand was a letter from her lover stating that he would not be back for Christmas.

"I think she's supposed to represent the woman who seems like she has everything, but she herself feels like she has nothing."

"What does that have to do with Christmas?"

"Well, I think it speaks to the fact that for some people, Christmas can be a very lonely time of year. It's hard to be single during a holiday that emphasizes family."

"You sound like you're speaking from experience," he said.

She had not expected such a personal comment and it caught her off guard. "I guess so. There are times when I wish that I had a husband and kids like some of my friends. Times when I can't shake the feeling that I'm missing out on something."

"I think that's human nature, though, isn't it? To wonder if perhaps the grass isn't greener?"

"You feel that way, too?"

"Sure. Sometimes even I wish that—"

"You had someone to kiss under the mistletoe?" she said before she could stop herself. She winced. "What am I saying? You've got plenty of women to kiss under the mistletoe."

"I know what you mean," he said, hurrying to her defense. "And the answer is yes. Sometimes even I wish that I had someone to kiss under the mistletoe. Someone that I loved."

She appreciated Rick making such a personal admission. He may be a pirate, but it was becoming obvious that he still had a heart.

As they stood there, they were joined by a couple carrying a Christmas tree. Off to their right, a young boy sat on his father's shoulders as he hugged a bag from FAO Schwarz.

"Are you done with your shopping?" she asked Rick as they turned to the corner.

"I haven't started. But usually I just give gift certificates. What about you?"

"My aunt is always complaining about the cold, so I got her a cashmere sweater and scarf."

Lessa stopped. The Rockefeller tree, sparkling with thousands of tiny multicolored lights, stood before them. "Do you mind if I take a closer look?" she asked, nodding toward Rockefeller Center. "I don't usually walk this way."

"I'm in no hurry," he said.

"Are you too cold?" she asked. "I'd be happy to give you back your coat."

"I'm just right," he said, taking her arm as they crossed

the street. It was the protective gesture of a gentleman, but suddenly there was an electrical current in the air. Something had shifted between them. By that subconscious response, they had gone from co-workers sharing a stroll to a man and woman sharing an evening out.

They walked to the edge of the street balcony and looked down on the skaters below. Despite the rain, it was a beautiful scene. The giant Christmas tree, the skaters, the shoppers, all framed against a background of sparkling lights. She inhaled deeply, smelling air redolent with fresh pine and roasted chestnuts. "I love this time of year," she said quietly.

He smiled. "Follow me." He took her hand and led her into the building beside them.

What did he have in mind? He glanced at her and winked as the guard got approval for them to enter. Rick led her to the elevator and pressed the button for the top floor. When the doors opened, he led her down a hall to the stairwell. "Where are we going?" she asked.

"Up," Rick said, climbing the stairs. "A friend of mine owns this building. Every year he has a Christmas party on the roof." He reached the top and opened the door.

She followed him out and stopped. Rockefeller Center, lit up in all its holiday glory, was directly in front of them. "It's beautiful," she said, impressed that he had taken the time to show it to her.

He moved closer, holding the umbrella over her head. Their eyes locked. After a moment's pause, he broke the trance and looked away. "I should get going."

"Me, too," she said. "I promised my Gran that I would bring back a tree tonight."

"By yourself?"

"I always do it by myself."

"I guess I shouldn't be surprised. If any woman is capable of carrying a tree home by herself, it's you. Come on," he said, taking her arm. "Let's go get that tree. There's a place I know on Lexington. It's a short walk from there to your apartment."

"But what about your car—" she said, surprised by his offer.

"I'll come back for it."

"You don't have to help me."

"I insist," he said. "Who knows? Maybe it'll help me capture some Christmas spirit."

"Then you have to take back your coat," she said, staunching his protests.

When they made their way back outside, Lessa stopped. The rain had turned to snow. "Look at this," she exclaimed excitedly as she stretched out her hand to catch a snowflake. "A perfect time to get a tree."

He put away his umbrella and, declining a cab, together they walked through the white-dusted world.

The Christmas-tree place could be seen and heard from a block away. "Here Comes Santa Claus" was playing over a speaker, and blinking, multicolored lights stretched from a lamppost to the greengrocer/tree store. A giant plastic Santa sat on the corner, smoking a pipe and watching over the festivities. Usually, picking out a tree was something Lessa did fairly quickly, as if knocking a chore off her list. But not tonight. Tonight she was more than happy to take her time. The salesman pointed to a fat evergreen and said to Rick, "Why don't you get your sweetheart the best tree we have?"

Lessa began to correct the man, but stopped. What

difference did it make if a stranger thought they were lovers?

Rick just grinned and said, "How about it, sweetheart?"

"If that's what you want, dear," she said, playing along.

Before she could stop him, Rick had bought the Christmas tree. "You didn't have to do that," she said.

"I have a secret motive. I wanted to get first dibs on the front. You take the stump," Rick said, holding on to the prickly part. "And lead the way."

Actually he had the tree more or less by the middle and was hefting the majority of the weight. "But you've got the worst part."

"First dibs, remember? No argument."

She smiled at his gallant act, accepted his kindness and started down the sidewalk.

"You usually do this by yourself?" he asked.

"I usually don't pick the biggest tree on the lot."

He laughed and raised it over his head to avoid hitting some fellow walkers. She knew the tree was heavy but Rick made it seem as light as a feather. Once again, she remembered the muscles she'd seen in his arms and torso. She had no doubt he was capable of carrying the whole tree and more. The shrill ring of a cell phone cut off her thoughts. "Hold on a second," Rick said, putting down the tree. He swung open his phone. "Hello." His voice visibly softened. "Yeah, I'm sorry about that. No, don't leave. Give my apology to your family. I'll be there as soon as I can."

She felt her heart drop. It was a woman, that much was obvious. And whomever she was, she was waiting for him with her family. Why had he told Lessa he wasn't seeing anyone right now? Had he lied to her?

"This is it," she said, nodding toward her brownstone.

She buzzed herself in and together they carried the tree up the flight of stairs to her apartment. The smell of pine filled the hall as her thoughts drifted back to the woman who had called, the one who was waiting for him. Lessa couldn't believe she had actually admitted to Rick that she wished for someone to kiss under the mistletoe. Regardless of what he had said, she doubted he was ever lacking a date under the mistletoe, love or no love.

She unlocked her apartment and led him inside. "Right in the corner," she said. The tree barely made it, skimming the ceiling. "Perfect," she said. "Now it feels like Christmas."

Rick's black cashmere coat was covered with needles. Without thinking, she brushed them off and said, "Thank you."

"I'll see you tomorrow," he said. Then he leaned toward her and for a split second she thought he was going to kiss her. Instead he brushed a piece of wet hair away from her lips.

It was an act of intimacy, a lover's touch. She forced herself to move, determined to mask her inner turmoil with a deceptive calmness. Too tongue-tied to say anything, she opened the door.

He smiled but there was something in his eyes that gave her pause. A sadness. With her heart in her throat, she said, "Have fun tonight."

Rick barely made it to the awards dinner in time.

"Where have you been?" Betty asked as he hurried though the door. "I thought you were going to be here at eight."

"I was…delayed."

"Delayed?" she asked, taking his coat and straightening his tuxedo tie. "I barely saw my family tonight. I missed our weekly dinner out because I was worried I wouldn't make it in time."

She had already told him that when she'd called. "I'm sorry," Rick said. "I ran into Lessa on the way out."

"So now it's 'Lessa,' is it?" Betty teased.

"She was on her way to get a Christmas tree," Rick said, ignoring her comment. "She needed help."

"Let me get this straight," Betty said, taking a step back and raising an eyebrow. "You were late to the New York Business Dinner because you needed to help Alessandra Lawrence get her Christmas tree? I'm shocked. You hate Christmas and everything surrounding it."

"This wasn't about Christmas. It was about helping someone."

"Surprise number two." She grinned. "You know, there's a rumor going around that you're falling for a certain chairwoman. I'm beginning to think there might be some truth to that."

Ever since he had returned from the Bahamas, he had been unable to stop thinking about Lessa. The woman he had gotten to know in the Bahamas was much more complex than the narrow-minded woman he knew from the office. He had seen her only occasionally since their return, but each time, his heart had soared. He had actually found himself looking forward to the office Christmas party simply because it would be an opportunity for him to spend time with her again.

When he didn't reply, Betty continued. "Unless it's

something else. You said you were determined to destroy her. Did you mean emotionally as well?"

Did Betty really think that he would seduce Lessa just to get revenge? "Is that what you think of me?"

"I know all about the fake romance, remember? And no one was around to see you picking out a tree. So what's it all about?"

"Am I up yet?" he said, glancing toward the stage as he checked his watch. He had been asked to announce an award.

"It's guilt, isn't it?" she said, ignoring his question. "She fell for you and now you feel guilty. And you should, too. Everyone knew she had a crush on you when she was young. You were her first love. I'm sure she's confused right now, poor thing."

"Poor thing? Just a week ago you were worried she was going to fire you."

"Well, she didn't. And she didn't even manage to fire you either. I just think she bit off more than she could chew. And now she's fallen in love with the man she thought she hated. She's probably imagining a romantic Christmas with you and her snuggled in front of a fire, and instead—"

"Betty," he said sharply, stopping her. "It's only been a week. She's not confused. She's got a lot of confidence. She's fully aware that this truce between us is only temporary."

"She may be saying that, but her actions proved otherwise, right?" She crossed her arms. "I can tell you right now that a Christmas tree is not going to be enough. If you feel bad about her getting her own tree, I can't imagine how you must feel taking away her company."

"I wish there was some other way to handle this, but there isn't."

Betty hesitated and said, "So you're going through with this?"

He didn't have to ask what she meant. He knew. Could he really destroy Lessa? "There's no choice."

Eight

She had just finished slipping her new red velvet dress over her head when Lessa heard a knock on the door. She glanced nervously at her aunt and said, "He's here and I'm not ready."

"Take your time," her aunt said, cracking her knuckles. "I'm looking forward to meeting this Rick Parker."

Her aunt's gracious words didn't fool Lessa. She knew that her aunt did not trust Rick, nor did she approve of her niece spending time with him...even if it was for the sake of Lawrence Enterprises.

"Be nice," Lessa pleaded. "Please. Remember, he is responsible for the biggest tree you've ever had."

"I just have a few questions for him," she said in her sweetest, little-old-lady voice.

Lessa yanked a pair of stockings out of her dresser. How had she gotten so far behind schedule? She had left work promptly at five, hurrying to the store to buy a new dress for the party. But she had made one simple mistake: She had taken her aunt with her. And when her aunt had asked to stop at Rockefeller Center to see the tree and the skaters, Lessa had been unable to say no. Nor had she been able to say no when her aunt had mentioned that she was getting hungry and had asked if they could stay for tea. Lessa had had the feeling that Gran was half hoping that Lessa would miss her date altogether.

She finished pulling on her panty hose as she heard the elderly woman say, "You must be Rick Parker. I'm Virginia Lawrence. My friends call me Ginny but you can call me Virginia."

Oh dear. "Rick!" Lessa called out. "I'll be right there."

She grabbed a brush and ran it through her hair. Then she thumbed through her makeup drawer, looking for a lipstick.

But Gran was just getting started. "I'm the aunt of your old boss, the man you fired, and the great-aunt of your new boss, the one who fired you."

Lessa grabbed the lipstick and swiped it across her lips. Good enough. "Sorry for keeping you waiting," she said, practically jumping into the foyer.

"No problem," Rick said. "I was glad to have an opportunity to meet your aunt."

Gran smiled sweetly, but she didn't fool Lessa for a minute. Lessa knew she had her talons out and was ready to let it rip. "Don't wait up," Lessa told her.

"You'll see her home tonight," her aunt said to Rick, as if placing a demand.

"Of course," Rick said.

She turned back toward Lessa and said, "Try and have some fun dear," as if she knew there was no possible way Lessa would be able to do that.

"Maybe you could make some cookies or something while I'm gone," Lessa said with a wink. "Something grandmotherly."

"Maybe I could give you a good kick in the—"

Lessa shut the door before Gran could finish.

"She's very funny," Rick said.

"I don't know about funny but she's feisty. I'm sorry if she was insulting."

"I can't say I blame her. After all, she thinks I fired her nephew."

"You did fire her nephew."

"Lessa," he said with a hint of exasperation as he led her to his car. She had expected something flashy and she was mildly relieved to see he drove an SUV. As she climbed inside, she couldn't help but wonder how many other of his women had sat in the very seat she was in. He climbed in beside her and shut the door. "We've been over this. I didn't fire your father."

She was not anxious to start this argument again. Not right then, at the start of their fake date.

He sighed and she knew he was not going to let it drop. "I was traveling almost nonstop back in those days. I had no interest in office politics. One day, I got a message stating that your father wanted me to return immediately. When I got back, he told me that he had heard from a reliable source on the board that some members were unhappy with his performance. He said he had even heard they had already picked out a successor. He asked me what

I knew, and I told him. Nothing. No one had spoken to me about getting rid of him or replacing him. That night I got a call from Ward Harding. He said that the board had voted and it was unanimous. They had fired your father."

Lessa glanced out the window at the thought of the pain her father must have felt. Ward Harding had once been one of his closest friends. "Only then did Ward ask if I would be interested in replacing your father."

"And you said yes."

"No. I needed time to think about it. I liked the travel and I had no desire to get swept up into office politics and become a manager. But when I found out what they planned on doing to your father, breaking their contract and giving him only a pittance of what he deserved, I felt I had no choice. Assuming the presidency was the only way I could help him."

She would have liked to believe that Rick was totally selfless and that his assuming the presidency had been a personal sacrifice, but try as she might, it was a hard nut to crack.

"Believe it or not, that's the truth," he said, his blue eyes radiating sincerity.

One thing was clear. She *wanted* to believe him.

"He thought you lied to him. That you were the one who convinced the board to fire him."

"He needed someone to blame. And he preferred me to his oldest and dearest friends."

She thought about the uptight, stuffy board over which she now presided. Ward, Franklin, Constance, John, men and women she'd known since childhood. And she wanted to throttle them.

But it was the night of the Christmas party. She

wasn't about to ruin it by picking a fight with an old, opinionated and ridiculous board member. She had to change the subject. She had to prepare mentally for the task ahead of her. After a few moments of uncomfortable silence, she said, "By the way, I really appreciate what you did last night, helping me with the tree."

"It was my pleasure."

"I hope you got to your date all right. She wasn't too mad at you, was she?" Lessa managed to say as nonchalantly as she could.

"My date?"

"I overheard you on the phone last night—"

"I hardly think a business dinner with Betty counts as a date," he interrupted.

"Betty?" Lessa felt a surge of relief. His secretary was the mystery woman?

"Of course. I always make Betty go to these functions and she always complains. As she is always reminding me, she doesn't need another man to take care of."

"What's the game plan for tonight?" Lessa asked, feeling suddenly refreshed, as if a weight had been lifted from her shoulders.

"Look, Lessa," he said, "I know you're not happy about this ridiculous pretend game. But I really think it will work."

How wrong he was. She was actually beginning to enjoy this game. "I hope so."

"Tonight I'm going to try and make this as easy for you as possible. I don't think we need to fall over each other. I think it's enough that we show up and leave together."

"Good," she said as enthusiastically as possible. How

could she tell him that she had been anxious for another opportunity to kiss him?

They drove the rest of the way in silence, until they pulled into the parking garage and he said, "Wait for me to open the door and help you down."

"I thought you said no open displays of affection."

"I'm not worried about what others might think. I just didn't want you falling out. It's kind of steep."

"I think I can handle it," she said. She thought back to Sabrina's story about how she'd met Rick when he'd carried her off the boat. He was obviously used to the fragile type. "I used to do plyometrics—jumping up and down off a step while holding a medicine ball."

He nodded toward her shoes. "In heels?"

Just to prove her point, she swung her door open and jumped out. "Can't pass up a dare, can you?" he asked, walking around to greet her. He took her arm and together they walked inside the building next door. Lessa couldn't help but notice the shocked looks on her co-workers' faces when they saw Rick's arm casually looped through hers. They endured a strained elevator ride up to the main floor of Lawrence Enterprises. It was crowded with office workers dancing to the live band and enjoying the free-flowing champagne.

"Looks like your party is a success," he said into her ear.

"It's in full swing," she agreed. Standing so close, she could feel the sexual magnetism that made him so self-confident.

"Can I get you something to drink?" he asked, as if he really were her date.

"White wine, please," she replied. He smiled at her and she felt her insides turn to mush.

"What was that all about?" her assistant asked, approaching her after Rick had left. "Did you come here with him?"

"Yes," Lessa said quickly.

Fran looked at her silently, as if waiting for her to continue. Lessa liked her but knew that she couldn't confide in her. There was too much riding on the whole scheme. But she couldn't lie to her either. And so Lessa said nothing on the subject. Instead she glanced around the room and said, "They did a good job with the decorations."

"After you left today," Fran said, "we heard from one of the buyers in Antigua. He's ready to make an offer."

Lessa felt a surge of excitement as she thought about the property in Florida. Her dream was one step closer to reality. "Great. I just need to run it past Rick," she said casually, trying to minimize the importance of his approval.

"I hope he's not furious," Fran said. "Antigua's his baby, his pride and joy."

"It's not a baby, it's a property. And Rick is a businessman. He'll appreciate all my research and my hard work."

Fran shook her head. "The last person who tried to do this without his approval got fired. But then again, they weren't *friends*," she said, emphasizing the word.

Lessa felt a hint of anxiety. She suspected Fran was only joking about him firing her. But he could make things unpleasant. After all, he had before.

She glanced around the room. Where was Rick anyway? Wasn't he supposed to be getting her a glass of wine? "I don't want to talk about business. How does everyone seem to be enjoying the party?" she asked.

Fran shrugged, as if she weren't impressed. "The shrimp is good."

After Fran had left to check out the desserts, Lessa headed toward the inner office staircase. The offices of Lawrence Enterprises took up the top five floors of a downtown building. In her attempt to make this party special, Lessa had spared no expense. Each floor had been decorated and had its own private bar. She walked up the ivy-lined staircase and found Rick outside his office, deep in conversation with the head controller. She was just about to make her way over to them when she recognized one of the senior board members flirting brazenly with a woman young enough to be his granddaughter. John Roberson was a nasty old man, one who had long been a thorn in her side. She glanced away, hoping to avoid eye contact. But it was too late.

"Look who's here," he said a loud and slurred voice as he made his way toward her. "The woman who single-handedly took ten points off our stock."

His remark had the intended effect. The crowd was stunned into silence. Lessa choked back her humiliation, aware that, once again, every eye was on her.

John slammed a big, fat finger into her chest and said, "Just because you studied history in school you think you're qualified to run a multimillion-dollar company?"

"Keep your hands off her," Rick said with a growl, stepping in front of Lessa.

"We made a mistake giving her the chairmanship," John said, his face red with anger. "The stock has gone down ever since."

"There were other factors at work."

"How can you defend her?" John asked. He shook his

head, disgusted. "Her father almost ran this company into the ground and apparently that's her intention as well."

And suddenly all the anger Lessa had felt regarding her father's shabby treatment burst to the surface. Her father had considered John Roberson a friend, yet according to Rick, he had betrayed him. "How dare you talk about my father that way," she said, clenching her fists as she took a step toward him. But Rick was too fast.

"Time to go," he said, grabbing John by the lapels and hoisting him away.

As Rick hustled John toward the elevator doors, Lessa glanced around at the crowd that had gathered to watch the fireworks. "Sorry about that, everyone. Go enjoy the party."

As the crowd slowly dispersed, misery set in. After all this work, what people would remember about the Christmas party was not the shrimp or the decorations or the fact that there was a bar on every floor. It was that the chairman of the board had almost punched a fellow board member. She made her way over to the bar and ordered a glass of wine. She had already drunk half of it by the time Rick reappeared.

"Thank you," she said.

He gave her a look that said all was not well. "Could I talk to you privately?" he asked.

She set down her wine and followed him toward a darkened hallway. Suddenly he pulled her into an empty office and shut the door. He turned on the light and faced her, his eyes dark and controlled. "Are you attempting to sell Antigua?"

"Not yet, no," she said calmly. "Although there is an interested buyer."

He took a step toward her. He was towering over her, his mouth set in a frown. "We're not selling Antigua. You've wasted your time."

"I found a property in Florida that has a lot of potential," she said, growing more uncomfortable by the minute. "It makes sense to sell Antigua now, before the other resorts on the island are developed. We could use the money to finance the Florida property. Anyway, I'm still getting my ducks in a row. I wanted to lay it all out for you."

"And what if I disagreed?" he asked. "We've ruined a relationship with whatever buyer you've strung along."

"I haven't strung anyone along. I told them exactly what the circumstances were."

She could see him hesitate.

"Let me show you what I've done. Give me a chance."

Before Rick could respond, the door flew open. The director of marketing entered arm in arm with the director of finance. When they saw Lessa and Rick standing in front of them, their jaws dropped in surprise. They moved away from each other. "We were just, um, looking for…some more napkins," the director of finance said quickly.

"So were we," Lessa said. "None in here." Rick followed her out.

"We can't talk here."

"Tomorrow morning. We'll discuss everything before I contact the buyer."

"Tomorrow morning won't work," Rick said. "I have a meeting that I can't change."

"Please, Rick, give me a chance. Let me prove to you that this will work."

He hesitated, looking at her sternly. She could almost see the inner machinations of his mind. "Then we'll do it now. Get your coat," he said. "I'll meet you downstairs."

Lessa found Fran on the second floor. "I have to go."

"You're going? You can't go! We haven't done the toast."

"You're going to have to take care of it. Rick and I need to discuss Antigua."

"You're *both* leaving?" she asked, her eyes widening.

"Yes, but—" But what? She couldn't very well deny an affair. So instead she shrugged her shoulders. "Thank you for taking care of things."

"Sure," Fran said, obviously stunned that the CEO and the chairman of the board would be leaving so soon and so together. "Have fun."

Fun, she felt like saying, was the last thing she would be having. She had never seen Rick so angry—not even when she'd fired him.

"All right," he said as they walked to the car. "Where to? Your place?"

Her place was not a good idea. She could just imagine trying to work with her aunt sitting at the table with them, making snide comments about Rick. "Your place," she said without hesitation.

Without saying a word, Rick turned the car toward his apartment.

Even though Lessa was the one who'd suggested that they go back to his apartment, Rick couldn't help but feel that this was a bad idea. It might have been okay if she weren't wearing a skintight red velvet dress that left little to the imagination.

But where else could they go? he asked himself defensively. Besides a restaurant, a coffee shop or any of the other million places that were available in New York City.

"How long have you lived here?" Lessa asked as they stepped inside the elevator in Rick's building.

He thought for a moment. "Five years."

Anger. He had to hold on to his anger. How could she presume to sell his property without even conferring with him first?

The doors opened directly into his apartment and they stepped out. He turned on the light. He took her coat, trying hard not to notice the curves beneath her dress. He hung up her coat as she walked over to the window and admired the view. She turned back to face him and asked, "Are you putting up a Christmas tree?"

"No. I never do. As I told you, I'm usually gone for Christmas."

"But you'll be in town this year," she said.

He would not allow himself to indulge in another personal conversation. It was too dangerous with them alone in his apartment. "Let's get to work, shall we?" he asked gruffly, nodding toward the table. She sat down beside him and began to talk.

An hour later, she looked at him and said, "Well? What do you think?"

He sat back, impressed. He had to admit that the proposal was not as farfetched as he'd initially thought. She had done her research. She understood the problem of the competing marketplace in Antigua as well as the potential and future worth of the property in Florida. "I'll take a look at this Florida property," he said after thinking it over. "Set up an appointment."

She smiled, obviously proud of her accomplishment. A lock of her hair fell over one eye and he had to stop himself from pushing it away. She may not have succeeded in convincing him entirely, but one thing was certain. He was not ready for her to go. He suddenly realized he was hungry. He hadn't eaten at the party and was fairly certain she hadn't either. "Are you hungry?"

"A little."

"I have a housekeeper who keeps me stocked with some basics. Or we can order in."

"Let's see what you've got," she said with a smile. He led her into the kitchen and opened the refrigerator door. She bent down and looked inside.

"Anything good?"

"You're right," she said. "Basics." She handed him a package of eggs. She put a block of cheese on top and grabbed a loaf of bread.

"Omelets?" he asked.

"No. I'm going to make a soufflé."

"A soufflé. Can you cook? I thought your aunt cooked for you."

"I've picked up a few tips along the way," she said with a smile.

An hour later, his apartment was filled with the warm, homey smell of fresh-baked biscuits and a fluffy soufflé.

When they sat down at the table, she waited for him to take a bite. "It's great," he said, eliciting a smile from Lessa.

There was something about her smile, something about the tenderness in her eyes that tugged on his heart. He felt a sudden surge of protectiveness, a desire to take her in his arms and protect her from the world.

And suddenly he remembered how he had felt when he'd made Karen smile. He could still see her laughing at the beach, her blond hair flowing in the wind. He had loved her with all the passion and naïveté of youth. But would their love have survived? If Karen had not died that day, would she still be beside him?

It was something he was ashamed to admit that he questioned. But how could he not? He had seen friends marry the woman they claimed to be madly in love with then file for divorce several years later. But, he reminded himself, those were his friends. He knew himself well enough to realize that he would never make the same mistake. When he fell in love again, it would be forever.

"Rick?" she asked and smiled. "Where did you go? You look so deep in thought."

"I'm sorry," he said. *Focus*. She was a business associate. The line was drawn. There would be no reprieve. But he couldn't help but wish otherwise. He remembered the way she had felt in his arms, the way she had looked up into his eyes. He had felt something, a stirring in his soul that he hadn't felt for years. But it was ridiculous. He could not have her. Never. His very career depended on it. "I should get you home," he said. "Your aunt will be worried."

"I'm not a child, Rick. I don't have a curfew."

What was that supposed to mean? "Just leave the dishes here," he said, standing. "The maid will take care of it tomorrow." He grabbed her coat and headed toward the elevator.

"Wait," she said, touching his arm. "Did I say something to upset you?"

How could he explain that he needed to get her out of there before he did something he would regret?

She stood in front of him, looking at him with her big emerald eyes. And then that damned lock of hair fell into her face again. But this time he didn't hesitate. He gently brushed it out of her face. And then she kissed him.

Nine

"I'm sorry," Lessa said quickly, breaking away. What was she doing? What had possessed her to kiss him like that? "I don't know what got into me."

But Rick did not look offended. There was electricity in the air as he gazed at her seductively. "Stay with me tonight," he said finally. He stepped toward her, trailing his hand down the side of her neck. She held her breath, closing her eyes as she enjoyed the delicious sensation. He tilted her head slightly upward, as if to kiss her. She felt her resistance fade away. He kissed her again, rough and hard. It was as if every part of her were on fire. She was powerless to do anything but give herself to him.

He took his time, intimately exploring her mouth. His tongue tickled and probed, claiming ownership. She arched against him, craving more. She ran her fingers up and down his back, feeling the strength of his muscles underneath his starched cotton shirt.

Her brain had long ago stopped working. Lawrence Enterprises seemed like a name from a distant past. All that mattered was what she was feeling right then and there.

She inhaled slightly as his hands slipped under her dress. His fingers made their way up her legs and sides, lightly touching her lacy bra. She arched her back, silently begging for more. Within a second, he had unhooked her bra and, with one hand, he began to finger the soft, plump flesh of her breasts while the other hand lifted her dress over her head. As her dress fell to the floor, he dropped to his knees in front of her, kissing the bare skin of her belly, working slowly, taking his time. He gently pushed her back onto the couch. As she sat against the smooth leather, he moved over her, working his way toward her breasts. He freed her breasts and took her nipple in his mouth, gently sucking and kissing. In one smooth maneuver, he removed her bra and leaned over her. In the light of the moon, she could see him stare at her, his eyes gazing up and down her body as if committing her to memory.

He reached his fingers inside the waistband of her panty hose, carefully taking them off. Still looking into her eyes, he slid his fingers in between her legs and underneath her panties. A ripple of excitement surged through her as she arched her hips. His touch was as light as a feather as he made his way toward her most sensitive point. The pressure slowly increased as he continued with his most intimate massage. She closed her eyes and her body began to surrender. "Let it go," he whispered. "Let it go."

When the release came, he silenced her cries with a kiss and cradled her in his arms, kissing her ear and brushing the hair, damp with perspiration, away from her forehead.

But if he thought that one orgasm was enough, he was wrong. It had done little to quench her desire for him. She was consumed with what it might feel like to have him inside her, to feel his naked body against hers. To have him make love to her.

"Your turn," Lessa said, staring brazenly into his eyes.

She unbuttoned his shirt, kissing his chest as she went. As he shrugged off his shirt, she kissed his neck while running the flats of her hands over his bare chest and down toward his belly. Her fingers slid over the hardness inside his pants, then reached for the zipper. He grabbed her wrist, stopping her.

"Are you sure?" he asked.

She had never been so certain in her life. "I want you to make love to me," she said, looking deep into his eyes.

He paused, as if giving her another chance to change her mind. She gave a tug on his pants and he kicked them off.

Like a Greek god, his finely carved body stretched out beside her. Every muscle seemed taut, as if his whole body were tense with desire. She ran her finger over his lips, working her way down his chin and his chest. As she moved down his belly and toward his hard self, she could see him swallow, fighting for composure. She took him in her hands, wrapping her fingers around him.

"I want you inside me," she said. "Now."

Staring deep into her eyes, he pulled her down beside him and skillfully flipped her underneath him. She opened her legs and he gently put himself inside her. He slowly began to move, thrusting deeper and deeper. She buried her hands in his thick hair as he kissed her, his lips hungry and demanding. It was unlike any sensation she had ever felt. Her body filled with a lush feeling of pleasure as she submitted her heart and soul to a primitive power.

Still pushing himself deep inside her, Rick stopped kissing her, hoisting himself up so that he could look directly into her eyes. It was even more intimate than a kiss. It was as if he could see directly into her soul. She fought off the climax that was threatening, desperate to maintain the luxurious tension between them. As if reading her eyes, Rick smiled slightly, and she could see his muscles tense. It was a dare to see who would lose control first. He gave a final thrust and together they relinquished control, releasing their bodies to pleasure.

When Lessa woke up, it was nearly two in the morning and she was naked on Rick's bed, locked in his embrace. She was filled with a feeling of bliss, a sense that all was right in the world. And then, just as quickly, the bliss did a one-eighty and turned into remorse. What had she done?

She had slept with Rick Parker. And not just once either. Twice.

He moved slightly in his sleep, his hand brushing against her bare breast. And just like that, the bliss was back. She was half tempted to reach under the covers and start everything all over again. But that would be a bad idea. If she didn't get home soon, her aunt would start to worry. Of course, she thought optimistically, she could call her and tell her she was, um, detained.

But that was a really bad idea. Because soon it would be morning and she would be forced to endure the official "morning after," complete with awkward conversation and embarrassing attempts to explain their behavior. Better to leave on a high note.

She slid out from underneath Rick's arm and scooted slowly out of bed. She grabbed her clothes and tiptoed quietly into the other room. She called a cab and dressed as quickly as she could. She arrived home and was thankful to discover her aunt sound asleep. She crawled into bed, her head spinning.

She had spent so much time hating Rick Parker. How could so much change so fast? As much as she was tempted to explain her behavior as an aberration, the truth of the matter was that she had known exactly what she was doing and to whom she was making love. And she hadn't cared one iota. It had been worth every single orgasm.

After a nap and a shower, she headed back toward the office, eager to return to the normalcy of work. It was only six o'clock, yet she felt certain that a long, hard day was just what she needed to snap her back to reality. But as she made her way through the office, occasionally passing a half-empty glass of champagne, she couldn't help but feel a little sad the evening was over. Although she knew she shouldn't, she couldn't help herself from wishing she could go back in time. That she could once again feel the strength of Rick's arms around her and the emotional power of their lovemaking.

She stopped. There, standing in her office, leaning up

against her desk as if waiting for her, was Rick. His normally slicked-back hair was tousled and he was unshaven, wearing jeans and a black turtleneck. He had, she thought, never looked so good.

"Good morning," he said.

"What are you doing here so early?"

He paused for a moment and said, "I came looking for you." He sighed. "I have a meeting and I wanted to talk to you before everyone else arrived."

But she didn't want to hear any I-don't-know-what-got-into-me excuses. That was exactly the reason she had left so early.

"Look, Rick," she said, raising her hand. "Let's not make a big deal about this. It happened. Let's just forget about it."

She thought she saw him hesitate. That was what he was going to say, wasn't it? She felt like kicking herself. Why had she cut him off? Why couldn't she just let the man speak?

"Forget about it? Is that what you want?" he asked.

"Yes," she said as confidently as she could, flashing him her best all-business smile as she sat behind her desk. "I thought I'd try and set up a look-through at Mara del Ray later today," she said, referring to the Florida property she had told him about. "I figure including air time, it would take us about eight hours."

"I don't think so."

"Rick, if you're worried about what happened last night, you don't need to be. It was just one of those things, a one-night stand, so to speak. We got it out of our systems and now we can move on." She tried to sound as casual as she could.

"It's not that," he said.

Well then, what was it? Was he still mad at her about Antigua? "I thought we worked out our difficulties last night. You said you were willing to look at the property and we have to do it today. I don't want to risk losing the buyers for Antigua."

"Look, Lessa. I have…another commitment this afternoon. A personal commitment. I can't make it."

Her heart fell. *Another commitment.* "What's her name?" she asked quietly.

He glanced toward her. "Her name?"

Normally she wasn't a masochist but, in this case, she couldn't seem to help herself.

He shook his head. "I don't have a date," he said. "Believe me, if that was the case, I'd cancel it. I have a family obligation."

She felt a sense of relief wash over her. *His family.*

He smiled and said, "My sister's getting married."

"On a Wednesday?"

"She wanted a Christmas wedding and it was the only time she could get the reception hall she wanted. It's a…well, a last-minute affair." He hesitated a moment and said, "Maybe you should come."

"What?" He wanted to introduce her to his family?

"Makes sense. The wedding's in White Plains at two o'clock. There's an airport in Westchester. After it, we'll leave directly for Florida. We should get there before sundown."

"I'd love to, but—" She hesitated. "Do you think it's a good idea? How's your sister going to feel about you bringing a co-worker to her wedding?"

"She knew she ran a risk having her wedding in the

middle of a work week. She'll just be happy that I'm there."

She saw herself surrounded by his devoted and loving family, all asking the same questions: Who are you and what are you doing with Rick?

"It's business," he said, summing it all up.

He made it sound so simple, as if meeting his family would be the most inconsequential event of the year.

Ten

Lessa arrived home shortly after lunch. She had given herself less than a half hour to get ready for the wedding and throw some items into a bag on the off-chance they ended up staying over. It was a time squeeze, but she had no choice. Her aunt had a lunch date and Lessa wanted to arrive home after she was gone so that she could postpone the confrontation she knew was coming. After all, she would have to confess her love affair to her aunt. She couldn't keep something that big a secret.

Unfortunately for her, Gran's lunch date had been postponed and she was still there when Lessa got home. As Lessa hurried to get ready, her aunt took a seat on the bed and wasted no time starting her interrogation.

"Well?" Gran asked impatiently. "I want details."

"The party was a bust. I certainly tried, but it doesn't seem to do much good." She pulled her blue dress over her head and said, "Sometimes I think I'm fighting a losing battle. I don't think anyone will ever see me as anything more than Howard Lawrence's daughter."

"You have to prove yourself."

"I haven't done a very good job so far. A board member accused me in front of everyone of destroying the company and I almost took him out. Nothing like punching an old man I could've blown over by whistling."

"Fire him," her aunt said defiantly, crossing her arms.

"I can't go around firing people. That's not going to solve anything. I think it was a mistake to fire Rick."

"I'm sure you do." Her aunt shook her head as she continued, grumbling, "You arrive home all disheveled at two in the morning. I wasn't born yesterday, you know."

"All right, here's what happened," Lessa said resignedly, taking a seat next to her. Whether she liked it or not, her aunt deserved an explanation. "During the party, Rick found out about my proposal to buy Mara del Ray. He was pretty upset so I volunteered to go over it with him."

"At his place?"

"We couldn't come here, you were sleeping. And the party was still going on at the office."

"So you went to his place."

"And…one thing led to another."

"You're not a virgin anymore?" her aunt asked calmly.

"Gran, I'm twenty-six years old. I haven't been a virgin for a long time."

"Tommy Winston?" her aunt said with a grin.

"Tommy Winston? No! I was in seventh grade when I dated him. We didn't even really date." In reality, she'd lost her virginity when she was in college, at the ripe old age of twenty-one, with Kevin Blane. He had been a popular fraternity boy with whom she'd had little emotional attachment. She had endured the whole thing with a let's-get-it-over-with attitude. They had slept together exactly twice.

"So now Rick wants to take you home to meet his family?" Gran asked. "Sounds serious."

"It's not like that. It only makes sense. I want him to see this property before sunset."

"And you couldn't take separate flights and meet him there?"

Gran had a point. "But there's only one corporate jet," Lessa said.

"So? You take the corporate jet and make him fly commercial."

"We need to go over everything first."

"I thought you did that last night."

"We discussed selling Antigua last night."

Her aunt raised her hands as if admitting defeat.

Lessa sighed. "It's no relationship, Gran. I don't think he's capable. And I know I'm not."

"You don't know that at all. You've never been tested. That's the problem. I always thought you were picky, just waiting for the right guy. Not the wrong one."

"I'm sorry, Gran. I know this seems strange. I spent all that time plotting revenge and thinking about how I was going to get rid of him. I hated him."

"There's a fine line between love and hate."

"I never thought this would happen. But I'm going to try and keep it all in perspective. I have to. I could be working with him for a very long time and I can't afford to be jealous or distracted."

"How in the world do you plan on preventing that?"

"I just can't allow it. That's all there is to it."

"I don't want you to take this the wrong way, Lessa, but how do you know that Rick didn't do this just to confuse you?"

"You think he slept with me just to bring me pain?"

"It's a possibility. It's also a possibility that it meant nothing to him."

"I don't think he did it out of spite, Gran. I know how I must sound, but he really isn't a bad person. Underneath it all, I think he's sweet and sensitive."

"I hope you're right, Lessa. I really do."

"I'm a big girl, Gran. I can take care of myself."

"You're going to have to if you insist on playing with pirates."

Normally, he would've been relieved to wake up and discover that his lover from the previous evening was gone. But not this time. It had only made him crave her more.

How had that happened? After all, Lessa was opinionated, stubborn and one of the most frustrating women he had ever encountered. But the truth of the matter was that underneath her bravado was warmth and tenderness. She had made him feel things he'd never thought possible again.

And so, when the opportunity had presented itself, he could not deny his mind or body the pleasure. But he would have to. As much as he was tempted to pursue their relationship, he had to agree with her. They would put the previous evening behind them. This was the only solution. After all, he was on the verge of winning back his company and firing her. As much as he might wish otherwise, Lessa did not belong at Lawrence Enterprises. She was resented and distrusted. The board would never again allow her any independence.

Although she was certain to be furious with him when she discovered that she had lost the company, in the end, he had no doubt she would be happier. She could take the money he paid her for her shares and start her own company. She would move on with her life, as he would with his.

But before then, he was going to introduce her to his entire family.

He must be crazy. After all, only a crazy man would do something so ridiculous. But it only made sense, right? They needed to go over their briefs before the meeting. They could do that on the plane.

Yeah, right.

The truth of the matter was that, like or not, he cared about Lessa. And, although they had promised each other that it was a single night, he was already longing for the moment when he could touch her again, when he could make love to her once more. He was not willing or able to go back to business as usual.

"Hello, Rick," Lessa said as she opened the door to her apartment. She looked beautiful. Her long hair was swept up, away from her face. She was wearing a blue dress that alluded to the beautiful curves underneath. "Come on in," she said, motioning for him to follow.

He glanced around nervously. "Where's your aunt?"

"She's not here. She went out to lunch with some friends."

He entered and shut the door. In the foyer, he looked

at the wall of pictures. They were old family photos featuring Lessa and her father. At the top was a picture of Howard with his arm around a woman who looked very similar to Lessa.

"That was my mother," Lessa said. "That was taken at El Vitro, their first property."

"Your mother was beautiful," he said. "She looks a lot like you."

"Thanks." She pointed out another picture. "There they are with me outside of my father's office. That was the day he incorporated Lawrence Enterprises."

From the pictures, Rick could almost feel his deceased boss giving him the evil eye.

Lessa put on her coat and grabbed an overnight case from beside the door. "Ready."

"Are you planning on staying a while?" he joked, nodding toward her bag.

"No," she said quickly, embarrassed that he might think she was plotting to get him alone. "After our last trip, I wasn't leaving anything to chance. I prefer my own swimsuit, thank you very much."

"I thought that other one looked kind of nice."

"Thanks," she said uncomfortably, ushering him out the door and down the hall.

They didn't speak until they were seated in his car. She asked, "So do you like the guy your sister's marrying?"

"Sure," he said with a shrug.

"You don't seem that happy about it."

Not happy about it? The truth of the matter was that his sister had suffered a nasty divorce that had been finalized only months before she'd met her new fiancé. Rick thought she was a fool to open herself up to more pain, but she was determined to be with her new love. And he gave her credit. "It's her business."

"Not a very romantic thing to say on the way to the wedding."

"Maybe not. But it's practical. She's been married before. You wouldn't know it though. She's going all out for this."

"She hasn't given up on love."

"Or maybe she'd just a glutton for punishment. She should've learned her lesson the first time."

"Does she seem happy?"

"That's how most relationships begin, don't they?" There were exceptions, of course, like his and Lessa's. They had begun as unhappily as most marriages end. What did that say for them?

They rode the rest of the way in silence, talking only when necessary. When they got to the chapel, Rick ushered Lessa past his stunned family, not stopping to introduce her. When he went back into the lobby, his sister said, "*You* brought someone? You actually brought a girlfriend to a family event?"

As a groomsman, Rick was required to work the crowd, seating people on either side of the church. Every now and then, he found himself glancing back toward Lessa. She seemed to be totally relaxed, busying herself by making conversation with the elderly woman next to her.

After the ceremony, Rick barely had time to say hello to Lessa before being whisked into the family photo session.

"I'll meet you at the reception," Lessa said.

An hour later, Rick and the rest of the wedding party

finally made their way across the street to the reception. As the bride and groom made their grand entrance. Rick scanned the room, looking for Lessa, but it soon became clear she wasn't there. He finally found her in the hall, helping an elderly woman out of the ladies room.

"This is Rick," Lessa said, introducing him to the woman.

"Oh, your wife has been so sweet to help me," she said. "I don't know what I would've done without her. My daughter was late and—"

"Here I am, Mom," a woman said, hurrying into the hall. She thanked Lessa profusely as she took hold of her mother's arm and helped her the rest of the way.

"Wife?" Rick asked when they were out of earshot.

"It was a misunderstanding. She knew I came here with you and she just made an assumption. I didn't see any reason to correct her."

"Look," he said, "I just have to stay for a little bit longer—"

"And who is this?"

Rick turned to see his parents were standing behind them.

"This is Lessa Lawrence," he replied.

His mother smiled and held out her hand. "How nice to meet you, Lessa."

"Lawrence," said his father, shaking her hand. "Any relationship to Howard Lawrence?"

"I'm his daughter."

"You're the one," his mother said, then looked at Rick. It was obvious by his mother's confusion that the only thing she had heard about Lessa was that she was a pain in the neck. Lessa smiled sweetly.

Rick felt the need to explain. "Lessa and I have a meeting later on. It makes sense to bring her here."

"I see," his father said. "Well, welcome, Lessa. It's very nice to meet you. You're so much younger and prettier than I imagined. Rick, you didn't do her justice." His father winked. "He told me you were pretty but he didn't say you were a knockout."

Her heart did a little flip as Rick winced. Rick had told them she was pretty?

As his parents walked away, Rick looked at his watch. "I think it's time to go."

"Don't be silly," she said with a smile. "We haven't even eaten yet. Besides, you don't have to entertain me. I'm perfectly fine by myself. Go be with your family."

A woman in a red bridesmaid dress came barreling their way. "Rick? Rick Parker! How have you been? I'm Jane Turner, remember?"

Rick shot the woman a grin that Lessa recognized immediately. Rick had no idea who the woman was.

"Would you dance with me?" she asked.

He glanced at Lessa, looking for help.

"Oh," the woman said, her face dropping. "Is this your date? I'm sorry. I thought your sister said you were coming alone."

"I'm not his date," Lessa said quickly. She turned to Rick. "Go ahead. Take your time. I'm fine."

Giving her a pained look, he walked to the dance floor with Jane Turner. Lessa went to the ladies' room and found Rick's newly married sister in there alone, struggling with her dress.

"Let me help," Lessa offered.

"You're Rick's date," Susan said with a smile. "I'm

so glad he brought you. How long have you two been seeing each other?"

"Actually, we're not really seeing each other. We work together. We have a meeting later today and it made sense to go directly from here." Before his sister could say anything, Lessa added, "I'm so glad I could be here, though. It was a lovely wedding."

"You're not seeing each other?" his sister asked suspiciously.

"Not technically."

His sister laughed. "Technically, huh? I saw the way he was looking at you. He appears quite smitten."

"We've only spent a couple of days together."

"So? I only met my husband three months ago. My mother married my father only six weeks after meeting him. Fast courtships are a family tradition. When Rick was engaged before, he proposed after only…" Her voice trailed off as she looked at Lessa. "You did know he was engaged before, right?"

Lessa nodded.

Susan smiled. "You see? I knew you were special. He must really care for you if he told you about Karen." She sighed and said, "We were all so worried about him after Karen's accident. He just withdrew from everything. Fortunately, he found that job. It was just what he needed. Or at least we thought so at the time. With him traveling to all those exotic locales, we felt certain he'd come home one day with a bride. But he hasn't dated anyone seriously since."

"Really? His reputation is as such a Don Juan."

"Oh, yeah. And he is, don't get me wrong. But I don't think all these casual relationships are what he really wants. He's like a nomad, wandering the earth. He's never around for family birthdays or holidays. He just gives a hundred percent to his job." She squinted her eyes. "Lessa Lawrence... Wait a minute. Aren't you the one who fired him?"

Uh-oh. "Yes. I was... well, not happy with what happened to my father."

"Rick felt bad about your dad. I remember him talking about it. But I don't think he had much to do with it, if that makes you feel any better. He told us that they were going to fire him whether or not he took over."

"I'm not sure of the details," Lessa said. She didn't want to get into this with his sister, that was certain.

"I bet you can find out. A lot of the board members are still there, right?"

They were and Lessa had done her best to check Rick's story. The board members she had spoken to had all told her the same thing. If Rick hadn't been there, they wouldn't have fired her father. "I would like to believe that he didn't have much to do with it," Lessa said. "But the truth of the matter is that he didn't stop it either."

"Did he have the power to stop it?" his sister asked. "From what I remember, they had already made their decision by the time they told him." She took Lessa's hand. "In any case, please don't hold it against him. I know he didn't want to hurt your father, or you, for that matter. He was numb back then, still reeling from Karen's death. Maybe he shouldn't have taken the job, but we all make mistakes, don't we? I've made my share." She leaned forward and said conspiratorially, "I was married before. It didn't work out, though. Have you ever been married?"

"Me?" Lessa laughed. "No."

"What's so funny?"

Why was she laughing? Because she had not even had a serious boyfriend. She couldn't very well go from not dating to getting married. "The concept of me having a serious boyfriend is funny, I guess."

"You and Rick sound like you're perfect for each other."

"I'm not like Rick," she said quickly. "I have the opposite situation. I rarely date."

"But you're dating Rick."

"Am I? I don't think so."

"You're dating. You're here, aren't you? I would bet you that he cares about you more than he's admitted. He never brings anyone to meet us."

"But we have to go to Florida—"

"Mumbo jumbo. He's had other meetings and inconvenient family obligations. He still never brought anyone."

There was a banging on the door. "Susan?"

"That's my husband," she said, her eyes lighting up. "Isn't he cute? Have you met him?"

"Yes. He seems very nice."

"Susan?" they heard again. "What in the world are you doing?"

She smiled and grabbed Lessa's hand. "Come on. Let me introduce you to the rest of the family."

Rick sat at the table, nervously looking around for Lessa. He had a feeling she was in trouble, and his fears were confirmed when he saw her arm in arm with his sister. He watched as Susan took Lessa's hand and proceeded to lead her smack into a group of cousins, introducing them one by one.

Rick's younger brother saw the interaction and laughed. "We're all intrigued by your mystery woman. Why didn't you tell us you were bringing someone?"

"Because I didn't realize it until this morning. And besides, she's not a date. She's a coworker."

"Sure," he said sarcastically. "This is me, Russell, your brother. I don't need the party line. Now, how long have you been seeing her?"

"She's the chairman of the board."

"Kind of young to be chairman of the board."

"My sentiments exactly."

"She's beautiful. And smart. And rich." Russell glanced at Rick again. "And she's not yours?"

"I already answered that question."

"So…you don't mind if I ask her to dance?"

"No," Rick said, his jaw tightening.

Susan came over, pulling Lessa by the hand. "Lessa and I were just getting acquainted."

"I think it's my turn," Russell said. He smiled at Lessa and said, "Would you like to dance?"

"I'd love to," Lessa said, accepting his arm.

As his brother led her to the dance floor and the two began moving to the music, Rick couldn't help but notice the way Lessa was smiling at Russell, as if she were actually enjoying herself. And his brother… Well, hell, he looked like he couldn't be happier. And why wouldn't he be? Rick remembered the way it felt to hold Lessa in his arms, to have her delicate arms wrapped around his neck. The way her breasts had felt against his chest.

Out of the corner of his eye, he saw his sister looking at him suspiciously. "Nice wedding," he said.

"I hope you like it," she replied. "It's my last one."

"I don't know," he teased. "Seems a shame to stop.
You're just getting the hang of it. This was so much better than the first one."

"Very funny. But it's your turn next."

He laughed. "I don't think so."

They were quiet for a moment as he continued to
watch his brother dance with Lessa. What the hell were
they whispering in each other's ears?

"She's a beautiful woman," Susan said.

"What? Oh, yes. Attractive."

"She certainly caught Russell's eye."

"So it appears."

The music changed tempo, slowing down considerably. But instead of leaving the dance floor, Russell
pulled Lessa close and rested his cheek against hers.

"Just a coworker, huh?" Susan said, motioning toward Rick's fists.

What was he doing? He relaxed his fists. He had no
reason to be jealous. Lessa Lawrence was not his and
never would be. "More than just a coworker. She's
chairman of Lawrence Enterprises."

"Hmm," Susan said, smiling.

"What's that supposed to mean?"

"It sounds like you've got a Hepburn-Tracy thing
going on. An office love affair."

"You're wrong."

"I know you. And I can see the way you're looking
at her. You can't stop thinking about her, right? And I
assume you've…held hands, so to speak."

"Look," he said. "I can guarantee this relationship is not going to go anyplace. She's arranged to give me half her stock in the company once this takeover threat is aborted. What she doesn't know is that I'll then own more than her."

"So you're going to fire her?" Susan asked. There was no mistaking the horror in her voice.

He paused. That was what he was going to do, right? "Yes."

"Rick," she said, shaking her head, "it's Christmas."

"Look, if there was any other way… But there's not." He had gone over it every which way. The truth of the matter was that he had no choice.

"But you care about her. I can see it in your eyes. Why can't you work together?"

"It's complicated." He didn't want to discuss it anymore.

"This is so typical of you. Dating someone that you think is safe. You only like relationships that come with automatic brakes. Did it ever occur to you to get rid of the brakes? Maybe you could have the ride of your life."

"I think you better lay off the champagne," Rick said.

She rolled her eyes and shook her head, frustrated. After a pause, she asked, "Are you going to Mom and Dad's for Christmas?" Every year his sister attempted to get him to come home.

"I don't think so," Rick said, sitting at the table. "You know how I feel about Christmas."

"It would mean so much to everyone if you were there. I thought that perhaps this year things might be different."

"Nothing's changed," he said, his eyes drifting back

to Lessa. With relief. he noticed that they had stopped dancing and were making their way back to the table. "You know what I say—"

"Christmas is for families and kids. Yes, I know what you say. But you're part of our family. And we would love it if you came."

"Hey, Susan," Russell said as Lessa sat down next to Rick, "Lessa doesn't have any plans for Christmas. I told her that she and her aunt should come to our house."

She was going to his parents' house?

"It might be better if I didn't," Lessa said, meeting Rick's eye. "After all, Rick and I work together…."

"He's never there on Christmas anyway. And the more the merrier. Besides," Russell said gleefully, "if the tennis club is open you promised to hit some balls to me." He looked at Rick and shook his head with disbelief. "You didn't tell me she beat Korupova. I saw that match on ESPN2."

"Good for you," Rick said stiffly to his brother. He turned toward Lessa and said, "I know my mother would love to have you."

"Russell, come with me," Susan said. "I need to show you something."

"What?" Russell asked. "What's so important?"

"Now, Russell."

"My brother's a great kid, isn't he?" Rick asked after Russell and Susan had left.

"Kid? He's a year older than me."

"He seemed to really like you." Rick hesitated and then asked, "So are you going?"

"Going where?"

"Christmas at my parents. He asked you, didn't he?"

"It didn't seem like you wanted me to accept his invitation."

"As they said, I won't be there. I don't care what you do. Outside of the office, that is."

She became quiet. Right away he regretted what he'd said. How could he tell her that he did care? That he didn't want her going near his brother or any other man? That she belonged to him.

She raised her hands. "What do you want from me? To not talk to anyone? That's why you're upset, isn't it?"

"Don't be ridiculous," he said gruffly.

At that moment, a team of waiters began serving, and the table soon filled with fellow guests. As he attempted to enjoy his meal, Rick found himself looking at Lessa. Seemingly relaxed and happy, she regaled the table with stories of her tennis exploits. Several times, she glanced at him and smiled, causing warmth to spread through him.

He poured her champagne and picked up his glass as they toasted the happy couple. He found himself wondering if he would ever walk down this road. It wasn't that he had completely written off the idea of marriage. It was just something distant, out there, that he felt he would address when it hit him.

Lessa, however, was the type of woman who would not stay single for long. Some man, some lucky man, would find her, and when he did, he would never let her go.

What the hell was happening to him? They had shared one night. One damn night. Yet the vision of her was seared into his mind. He couldn't forget the way she had felt in his arms, the smell of her, the feel. He had only one option. He would go to Florida with her as agreed. And then he would stay the hell away.

Eleven

Located on the Gulf of Mexico, Mara del Ray had been built in the 1970s and had immediately become a leading resort, frequented by the rich and famous. But in the 1990s its allure had faded. Although still open for business, the present owner had done little in terms of upkeep and renovation. It was almost dark when Lessa and Rick arrived, but even in the dim light, it was obvious that the buildings were in need of paint and repairs. Some still had visible hurricane damage. But, as Lessa discovered, the property, although overgrown, was still lovely. A white sandy beach ringed with palm trees offered a spectacular view of the Gulf of Mexico.

"You have to use your imagination," she said after the owner had given them a tour.

Rick could see immediately why Lessa was interested. Although the buildings would need to be completely refurbished, the setting was one of the most romantic he had seen. But an Antigua, it was not.

He turned toward the owner. "Could we have a moment alone, please?" After the man stepped back, Rick said, "I don't think this property is going to work."

"Why not?"

"Because it's going to take a lot of money to get this place up to our standards. And where are we going to get the start-up capital?"

"From Antigua."

"I don't want to risk a known quantity on this."

"Perhaps we should take it back to the board and let them decide."

"You should know by now that the people on the board are no friends of yours."

"All right," she said, in an obvious attempt to be fair, "why don't you tell me what your concerns are so I can address them."

"I already did."

"This has nothing to do with Antigua, does it? This has to do with who's in charge."

"I'm all for picking up cheap properties and turning them around. Unfortunately, this property is neither cheap nor is it capable of being turned around."

"We're interested, " Lessa said, signaling the owner back over. "Very interested. But my partner and I have to discuss it further."

"We have two other bids," the owner said. "Not much time for discussion."

"It's hard to see in the dark," Rick said. "For all we know, this place could be falling down around us."

"Stay here tonight as my guests," the owner said. "In the morning you will see that it is every bit as beautiful as it is at night."

"There's an idea," Lessa said cheerfully.

It was an idea, but not a good one. "I can't," Rick said. "I have to get back."

"Please, Rick," she said. "Like you said, how can you make a decision when you can't see what you're buying?"

As he looked into her deep green eyes, he could feel his resolve fade. His phone rang and he flipped it open. It was Betty, calling with good news. Sabrina was ready to sell. He snapped shut his phone and said, "We heard from Sabrina. She wants us to meet with her tomorrow morning."

Lessa's face lit up. "We did it," she exclaimed, spontaneously throwing her arms around him. He held her stiffly, trying hard not to enjoy the feel of her body pressed up against him.

As if suddenly realizing what she was doing, she stepped back. "I'm sorry. I guess I got a little carried away."

"You have reason to be excited," Rick said. "Apparently Sabrina is also interested in this property. I have a feeling that when she heard you and I were coming to look at it together, it convinced her we were romantically involved."

"It's foolish to go all the way back to New York when we have to be in the Bahamas tomorrow morning," Lessa said. "It makes sense to stay here tonight. In the morning we'll give this property another look and then head over to see Sabrina."

Telling himself that he had no choice, he acquiesced.

They followed the owner back into the lobby. "I have the perfect room," the man said, grabbing a key at the front desk. "Facing the ocean. You will get a true feel for the resort."

"That's rooms," she said, correcting him. "We need two rooms."

The man looked at Rick. "But I thought—"

Rick shook his head. "Two rooms." As far apart as possible, he felt like adding.

They followed the owner down the hall and back outside, to a two-story stucco building located just steps from the beach. The owner slid the key into one lock and then another. "Adjoining rooms," he said, opening both doors at the same time.

"That's not necessary," Lessa said.

"Oh," the owner said, disappointed. "But these are the two best rooms."

"They'll be fine," Rick said, walking into his room. "Thank you."

He shut the door and immediately opened the adjoining door that separated the rooms.

"What are you doing?" she asked.

"I don't like you staying in here by yourself. We'll keep the door open."

"Rick," she said, "we agreed that last night was—"

"Believe me, Lessa, I have no intention of repeating anything. But I feel a certain…responsibility to return you to the company in one piece. Now," he said, turning the light on in the other room and setting up his computer. "We have some work to do. We need to track down the board and set up a meeting for when we return." He knew it wouldn't be easy. Most members had left town for the holidays and were spread out across the country at their various vacation homes.

He heard Lessa go into the bathroom. When the door opened, he glanced up and, as she walked past, he caught a glimpse of skin. A lot of skin. "I'll see you later," she called out.

He jumped up so fast he almost knocked his computer off the table. "Where are you going?" he asked, heading into her room.

"I'm going to take a quick swim," she said, wrapping a towel around her waist.

"It's not safe."

She rolled her eyes. "I'll be back soon," she said, shutting her door. He ran his fingers through his hair and rolled his neck. What the hell was happening to him? He sounded like a cross between a doting father and a jealous lover. What he didn't sound like was a businessman who was on a trip with a coworker.

But he didn't like the idea of Lessa walking along a deserted beach at night. He didn't care if they were in paradise, sometimes things happened. Some guy might get the wrong idea. And what about the water? Who knew what dangers lurked in there? More than one swimmer had been lost in a riptide. It was ridiculously stupid to go swimming by oneself.

And just like that, he was out the door after her.

It was nearly ten o'clock and the beach was deserted. It was a clear night and the sky was littered with stars. "Lessa!" He scanned the water, looking for her. Damn. Why had he been so pigheaded? It was he who would be responsible if anything happened to her. "Lessa!" he yelled again.

He saw her in the distance, swimming back toward shore. He felt a surge of relief as he picked her towel off the beach.

She stood up in the water, her long body glistening in the moonlight. He stood on the shore, watching her walk toward him. She looked like a beautiful mermaid come to life.

He had every intention of handing her the towel and heading back to the room. Instead, he gently wrapped the towel around her shoulders. She touched his cheek and then he saw the hunger in her eyes. It was all he needed.

Like a lit match to an oil slick, the passion he had been trying to hold at bay burst forth. With a hint of desperation, he pressed his lips against her, hungrily claiming what he desired. He ran his hands down the front of her swimsuit, feeling her nipples harden with his touch.

Suddenly, she broke away and stepped back. "I thought we agreed this was supposed to be a one-night affair."

"There's a problem with that whole one-night thing."

"Problem?" she said weakly as he kissed her long and slender neck.

"Well, there's a lot of problems with it," he said, and with that, he swept her up into his arms.

As he carried her back to the room, she relaxed against him, resting her head on his chest. He kicked open the door and set her down on the bed.

Her hair was tousled by the wind, her cheeks still flushed from his kisses. She looked beautiful and wild, a woman possessed with an almost ethereal natural beauty. Staring into her eyes, he slowly peeled down her suit so that he could caress her breasts. Her head tilted backward and she closed her eyes as he touched her. Within seconds he had her completely naked, her form illuminated in the soft light. He took a moment, his breath ragged as he took in the sight of her long legs and voluptuous curves.

She gingerly ran her fingers across the starched linen of his shirt. Looking him in the eye, she took on the role of temptress. She ran her hands down his front, a smile touching her lips as she pressed against the hard mound in his pants. She unzipped them and took him out, caressing him with her fingers.

Lessa knelt over him and guided him inside. She moved above him like a woman possessed, determined to seek her own pleasure. He watched her carefully, controlling his own desire until she inhaled sharply and her body trembled with release. Only then did he let himself share in the pleasure.

As Lessa kissed him tenderly, he wrapped her in his arms.

"What have you done to me?" he whispered. "What have you done?"

The next morning, Lessa woke up in a tousled mess of sheets. Unlike before, she felt no urge to sneak away. She was happy right where she was, nestled in Rick's arms.

"Good morning," he said, running his finger across her bottom lip.

"Morning," she said, nestling even deeper into the crook of his arm as she listened to the sounds of the hotel coming to life. A breakfast cart being wheeled past their room, a mother scolding her children. A shower was turned on; an alarm clock was turned off. In fact, she could hear…well, everything.

"These walls certainly aren't soundproof, are they?" she said.

"I'll have to sneak you out of this hotel after last night. I'm surprised no one called security."

She laughed and then fell silent.

"It's too late for regrets," he said.

"I don't have any regrets."

He kissed her on the lips. "I'm glad to hear that."

She leaned over him, glancing at the clock on the table. It was almost time to go. As if reading her mind, he said, "I guess we should get going."

"You first," she said, nodding toward the bathroom. "I just want to lie here for a minute."

He gave her a kiss and then, reluctantly, broke away. As she watched him walk into the bathroom, she couldn't help but wonder how long it would be before she saw a man naked again.

The pit in her stomach, the emptiness that was filling her heart…it was all about sex, right? No. The sex had been amazing, no doubt about it. But the impending dry spell would not cause this kind of pain. It was Rick she would miss.

She was suddenly overcome with sadness. She couldn't help but wish things were different. Wish that perhaps they had met under different circumstances. If they didn't each carry their own complicated baggage, would they have had a chance? She didn't know. The only thing she was certain of was that he was still there and still naked.

She heard the shower going and followed the sound into the bathroom, opening the shower door. His thick hair was slicked back. He looked like he was ready for a black tie affair, minus the tux and undergarments. He smiled his sexy half grin and held out his hand toward her.

She stepped inside. The water beat down as she ran her fingers up and down his naked and wet torso. She could see his shaft grow heavy as he pressed against her. He took the soap and slid it around her back, up and down her legs. He reached between her and fingered her as the warm water beat against them. Only when she thought she couldn't take it anymore did he lift her up and enter her, holding her against the side of the shower with his bare strength.

Afterward, he wrapped the towel around her shoulders and kissed her. "I'm liking this hotel more and more."

A knock sounded on Rick's door. "Mr. Parker? Are you ready for your tour?"

They dressed hurriedly and headed back outside. A steamy heat and the threat of a storm welcomed them. As they were led around the property, she couldn't help but notice the change in Rick. Perhaps it was their love-making or perhaps just the knowledge that Sabrina was ready to give them their shares, but Rick was joking, even laughing with the owner as he offered Lessa suggestions on ways they could improve the property.

As she walked by Rick's side, she thought about her parents and how they must have felt viewing their first property. It wasn't the same, of course. Rick, unlike her father, had been doing this for years and was at the top of his game. But this was her first property, the first one that she had discovered and wanted to buy, and she felt an excitement in the air. A big what-if.

And although, in the end, Rick did not agree to purchase the property, he at least agreed to consider it. She knew that whatever decision he made, she would have to trust him. For the first time ever, she saw a light at the end of the tunnel. He was her partner but he was also much more. He was her friend.

Twelve

As Rick watched the world disappear beneath them on the flight to the Bahamas, he thought about the previous evening and something became painfully clear: He could not take this company away from Lessa.

He had gotten too involved and there was no turning back. This was no simple affair. He could not hurt her.

So what should he do?

He had already bought the stock; their contract was signed a week ago. Once Sabrina sold him hers, he would automatically be the new owner of Lawrence Enterprises. He would then officially give Lessa back her stock and, at the board meeting, he would announce his support of her chairmanship. If Lawrence Enterprises was what Lessa wanted, it was exactly what she would get.

Their flight arrived shortly before noon. Sabrina had

sent a car and together they drove to her office, where Sabrina was waiting for them. She leaned over her desk in front of Rick, causing her cleavage practically to fall out of her shirt as she pretended to sort through some papers.

"Well, well, well. It's so nice to see you again."

"I can't tell you how happy we were to receive your phone call," Lessa said.

She raised an eyebrow. "I bet you were."

She motioned toward the chairs, encouraging them to sit. "Can I get you something? Tea? Coffee? Water?"

"We're anxious to sign the contract," Rick said.

"I have it right here," she said, waving it in front of them. "Before I sign it and we make this all official, I wanted to take a moment to congratulate you both on your ridiculous performance. Although I must say, Lessa dear, you were a little stiff. But your trip together to Mara del Ray was a very nice touch."

"I'm sorry?" Lessa asked.

"You, Rick, however, almost had me convinced. There was a look in your eye, one that gave me pause." She laughed. "But you, Lessa…I never quite bought it. Then again, you had a much more difficult job. After all, how could you take up with the man who ousted your father? But I was willing to give you the benefit of the doubt." She shrugged her shoulders. "I'm such a romantic at heart. And of course, everyone knows that for some, love is blind. Also, having tasted the goods myself, I know how, well, persuasive Rick can be." She stood before Rick and caressed his cheek. "And now that you got what you wanted, Rick, and you're through with Alessandra, perhaps you and I can rekindle what we once had."

Rick froze. Sabrina knew. "Sign the contract," he commanded. "Now."

"What's going on?" Lessa asked.

Sabrina looked at Lessa and flashed her an evil smile. "Is it possible she doesn't know what you've done, Rick?"

"I bought some shares, after you fired me," Rick said to Lessa.

"Some shares?" Sabrina said. "How modest."

"Things have changed since then," he said to Sabrina.

"I'm afraid you've been double-crossed, my dear," Sabrina said to Lessa. "But don't feel bad. I have all sorts of people working on this and I just found out myself this morning. Unfortunately it doesn't change much for me. Because once Rick gets your shares, he'll be quite invincible."

Lessa glanced toward Rick, as if looking for some sign of reassurance that Sabrina was making the whole thing up.

"Lessa," he said, "I have several other business ventures. Each one of them bought a significant share of stock during the period of time I was not working for Lawrence."

"Spell it out, Rick, for God's sake," Sabrina said. She turned to Lessa and explained, "Once he gets your stock he'll own the majority. Enough to wield significant control, like making himself chairman and CEO."

Lessa sat silent, her eyes blazing with the pain of betrayal. "You were going to fire me?"

What could he say? Until he'd gotten involved with her, he had hoped to do just that. But everything had changed. "Originally, yes. I felt as if I had no choice. But I've since changed my mind."

He could tell from the look in her eyes that she did not believe him. He wanted to take her in his arms and get her the hell out of there. To prove to her that he was sincere.

"Actually, Lessa," Sabrina interjected, "considering the recent turn of events, I'm hopeful that you and I might work out a deal. You only have to give him the company back if he prevents a takeover, correct? Which is dependent upon me selling you my shares."

And suddenly he saw where Sabrina was going with this. She wanted to take advantage of Lessa's emotions to try and talk her out of her stock.

"We're two women who have been betrayed by Rick," Sabrina continued. "Sisters in pain, so to speak. Sell me your shares. Give *me* the company instead of Rick."

Lessa appeared to hesitate. She couldn't really be considering this, could she? "Lessa," he began, "I didn't want to hurt you."

"He betrayed not only your father, but you," Sabrina said. She grabbed the contract and ran it through her fingers, as if ready to rip it to shreds. She walked over and sat on the edge of her desk, directly in front of Lessa. "I sign this and he gets the company. Sell me your stock instead and I'll give you the same deal you were going to give me."

"That's enough," Rick said angrily to Sabrina. He took Lessa's hand. "I had changed my mind. I wasn't going to go through with it. You have to believe me. When I bought that stock you'd just fired me. I had no other options."

Lessa pulled her hand away and closed her eyes, as if fighting back the pain.

How could he have allowed this to happen? The last thing he wanted was for her to get hurt. "I don't want your stock anymore. We'll renegotiate."

Sabrina's voice snaked in. "Desperate words from a desperate man. You can't possibly believe him, can you, Lessa?"

"You're right, Sabrina," she replied. "I don't want to give this company to him. But I don't have a choice. I can't bear the thought of you breaking it up and selling it off piece by piece." She took the contract out of Sabrina's hands and laid it on the table. She picked up a pen and handed it to her. "Could you sign this, please?"

Sabrina hesitated before finally signing. She begrudgingly handed the contract to Lessa. "You just lost everything," she said. "For what?"

But Lessa didn't answer. She walked over to Rick and handed him the contract. "You worked hard for this." And with that, she walked out of the room and out of his life.

How could she have been so foolish as to believe he really cared about her, to believe he would not betray her? And finding out through Sabrina only added to her humiliation. How could he have done this to her? Tears stung her eyes as she hurried toward the car. Just as she was about to get inside, she felt a hand on her arm.

"I need to talk to you," Rick said, steering her toward a private area by the beach. "This is a misunderstanding."

"A misunderstanding?" She shook her head sadly. "You warned me, didn't you?" It had been a brilliant yet simple plan. A trap that she had walked right into. Did she really think Rick would ever agree to be partners, especially with someone he held in such low esteem? Their affair had been nothing but a distraction for him, an opportunity that she herself had offered. She didn't blame him so much as herself. She had been a fool.

"When I bought that stock we were not involved," he said.

"But after we were involved you didn't tell me, did you?"

"I didn't see any point until I could prove to you otherwise."

"You planned everything, right down to your own firing. You pushed me into firing you just so you could buy stock. And then when I asked you back, you knew that you'd be able to get rid of me."

"And I planned on firing you just as soon as I got my company back. That's all true."

"Revenge," she said softly. She had fired him and he'd planned on doing the same thing to her.

"But that was before I got to know you. Before I began to care about you."

She desperately wanted to believe him. But how could she? It might be another lie. The more she thought about Rick and Sabrina, the more she felt they deserved each other. Sitting there in that office, the two of them had been wily and frightening, firing each other, sleeping with each other, making deals behind each other's backs. It made her sick. Maybe she didn't have the stomach for this business after all. She needed a little time to digest all that had happened to her and consider her next move.

"When people care about each other, they help each other," she said. "They look out for each other."

"I'm giving you back your stock," he said, as if that made everything all right.

"I don't want it back."

"I'll pay you for it. I'll pay a premium. Whatever you want."

She looked into his eyes, desperately searching for some sign of the man she had grown to care about. She wanted to believe him, believe that this had all been a colossal misunderstanding, but how could she?

"You don't get it, do you? It's not about money. It never was."

Thirteen

It was official. She was lost.

Lessa scooted forward in her seat as she drove slowly down the two-lane dirt road in Connecticut, hurrying toward a board meeting in the middle of nowhere. On either side of the road was a landscape more appropriate for Halloween than Christmas: deserted farmlands, their brown, dried-out grasses blowing in the wind. Every now and then she would see a lone abandoned house or barn with the roof caved in. Lessa followed the winding road down a hill and found herself enveloped in fog. She turned on her fog lights and continued, slowly making her way through the thick, cotton clouds. She had agreed to have the meeting at this out-of-the-way location because it was Christmas Eve and many board members were already at their vacation homes throughout New England. This just happened to be the halfway point. But the last thing she felt like doing on Christmas Eve was driving around dirt country roads in search of an ornery board and their deceitful, if charming, president.

At the thought of Rick, her stomach turned over. This would be the first time she had seen him since they had returned from the Bahamas. Despite his repeated phone calls over the past two days, she had not spoken with him. What was the point? He had her shares. Although she had been a fool, he had played by her rules. And she had lost.

And now she had no choice but to resign her position on the board. It was ridiculous to think that she could stay on. After all, she had never fit in with the stuffy and shortsighted people she was surrounded by, the same people who had fired her father. And now that she had lost her stake in the company, why would they keep her on? They would not. It was time to bow out gracefully.

Unfortunately, it was proving easier to walk away from the company she had thought she loved than it was to walk away from Rick. She had barely slept all night, filled with dread at the thought of seeing him again. Instead she had walked the floor, analyzing and reanalyzing the situation. She didn't need Psych 101 to figure out what had happened. It boiled down to one issue: honesty. This whole thing could have been avoided if she had just been honest with herself. After all, did she really think that Rick would agree to be her partner? Did she really think that just because he had made love to her he would fall in love? Rick had remained honest to himself and his business. It was she who was the traitor.

She had underestimated his immense attraction. With one kiss, Rick could make a woman forget who she was and where she was going. It was the way he listened, the way he looked at her when she spoke. He made her feel as if she were the most interesting person in the world.

Time, she thought. She just needed some time to clear her head before seeing him again. She needed some time to think before even mentioning his name. But she didn't have any time. In fact, according to her watch, the board meeting had already started.

She thought of the scene that awaited her. Were the board members eager to give her the evil eye? Would they jump with glee when she informed them she was resigning? Or did they already know? Some, she suspected, had been aware of Rick's plan from the beginning. She was on her way out, Rick was back in power and the stock was already going back up.

She checked her watch once again and pulled out her cell. Still no reception. A psychologist would have a field day with this one. She, who was never late, was going to be late for her own resignation. Was her tardiness intentional? And why wasn't she more upset about leaving Lawrence?

True, her time there had not been happy. She had been fighting an uphill battle, one that had been doomed from the beginning. The only reason she'd had even attempted it was because of her promise to her father. She had never asked herself whether being a part of Lawrence Enterprises again was something she really wanted, because it did not matter. It was an obligation, something she had to do.

But she'd always known her aunt was right; if Lessa had succeeded at Lawrence, she would have paid a steep price. Lawrence Enterprises was a public company and she knew from her father's experience just how taxing and emotionally exhausting it was to run. There would always be someone looking over her shoulder, someone trying to take her place.

Perhaps she should think optimistically. It was very possible that this was a blessing in disguise. She did not want to work for someone else. She wanted her own company run by her own rules. Unfortunately, the whole experience made her wonder whether had she chosen the right business. Was she destined for a career in the resort industry? She had always thought that if she worked hard enough, like she had in tennis, she would succeed. But she had had talent on the tennis court. Was it possible she had no talent for this business?

One thing was obvious—hard work alone was not enough. Perhaps, she thought optimistically, all she needed was a little luck.

As if the forces were listening, her car suddenly began to shimmy. She fought for control of the car, yanking the throbbing steering wheel and pulling over to the side of the road. With a groan of despair, she hurried outside to inspect the damage. So much for luck. The right wheel looked like a deflated inner tube.

Lessa glanced around the desolate area as she tied her scarf more securely around her neck. Although the fog had cleared somewhat, a cold and bitter rain still fell. She headed around the side of the car toward the trunk. Her only hope now was that she would find a spare. And figure out how to use it.

Rick had been looking forward to this meeting. Since their return from the Bahamas, he had struggled to focus at work. He was like a man possessed. Lessa haunted his thoughts and dreams. The board meeting at least would provide another chance to explain himself to her, another opportunity to prove himself. He would succeed, he had no other choice. He did not want their relationship to end, not like this.

What had gotten into him? After all, wasn't the inevitability of the relationship's demise what he'd found so attractive in the first place? Wasn't this his pattern? Hadn't his sister accused him of only getting involved with women who were "safe"? Women who, for obvious reasons, he could never love? He had done this ever since Karen had died.

But this time, something was different.

He had never met a woman like Lessa. She was brilliant, determined and feisty. Not to mention her obvious physical attributes. She was a classic beauty, with eyes that seared right through a man, the kind that haunted his dreams. But she was more than a compilation of superficial qualities. There was a vulnerability that he saw in her, a sweetness that made him want to protect her from the world.

Rick checked his watch again, then glanced around the table. The board was getting agitated. Where the hell was she? His heart filled with dread. What if something was wrong? What if something had happened to her?

No. That was ridiculous. He was certain there was a logical reason for her tardiness. He checked his watch again.

"Let's vote," Ward said. "I think we have a consensus anyway. We don't need her here to fire her, do we?"

"We're not firing her," Rick said quietly.

"You can't be serious," John said. "We're certainly

not going to keep her on the board. Why should we? After all, thanks to you, she's got a minority stake. And we all saw what she did to the company. She almost led us to ruin."

True, Rick had once thought the same thing. The stockholders had made it clear they did not consider Lessa an asset. But they didn't know her. They, like the board, had not given her a chance. "You're all forgetting that I now own a majority. And I say she stays."

The room silenced as everyone looked at him, their faces drawn and pale. "You can't be serious," Ward said.

"I am serious."

"She doesn't even have the courtesy to show up on time."

"Maybe something happened," Betty said quietly, voicing his own fear. The muscles in Rick's neck tensed as the color drained from his face.

Rick pushed back his chair. He couldn't take this any longer. He stood up and began walking toward the door.

"Rick?" Betty asked. "Where are you going?"

"I'm going to find Lessa," he said. And before anyone could protest, he left.

Lessa glanced at the mud surrounding the tire. How was she going to do this without becoming a big mess? In an attempt to protect her suit she took off her pretty wool coat and laid it smack in the middle of the mud. She knelt down, fit the tire iron on a bolt and twisted.

Nothing. The bolt didn't move.

Droplets of rain splashed mud on her clothes as she heaved the iron once again. But her efforts were in vain.

She took off her gloves, as if her bare hands might do better. She tried another bolt and then another. Finally, Lessa put down the tire iron and leaned back against the flat tire still on the car. The freezing rain pelted her face and the cold wind whipped through her drenched clothes. But she didn't mind the rain. In fact, it suited her mood just fine.

The distinct whirring of a car engine filled the air. At the sight of headlights, she jumped up, ready to flag down the motorist.

The car pulled beside her and stopped. Her heart caught in her throat as she recognized the vehicle. Rick? In a sudden stab of vanity, she smoothed her mud-spattered suit. She tucked her hair behind her ears and licked her lips.

The car stopped and Rick jumped out. He stood there looking at her, his brow furrowed in worry, his features dark and handsome. The mere sight of him was enough to make all her angst flood to the surface. And suddenly, whether it was the stress of the morning or simply the stress of seeing him once again, she felt like crying. She bit her lip, trying to gain control of her emotions. She could do this. It was almost over.

"What the hell happened to you?" he asked.

She motioned toward her car. "I got a flat tire."

"Why didn't you call?" he asked, looking at the tire.

"No cell service around here," she said, shivering.

He shook his head, his eyes scanning over her. Once again she was aware of how she looked, the mud-spattered suit, the motley hair. She crossed her arms as he approached. She had imagined this encounter many times in the past few days. Would she slap him and insult him? Or act cool and collected, as if he and the company meant little to her?

"What is it with you and coats?" he asked.

"I used it to kneel on. I didn't want to get dirty."

He took off his coat and attempted to loop it around her shoulders.

"I don't want your coat," she said, stepping away from him. She didn't want to touch him or anything that belonged to him.

She might as well have slapped him. His eyes darkened and narrowed. "Get in the car," he said.

She might not have wanted to touch him or anything that belonged to him, but she was willing to make an exception when it came to his car. She picked her wet and muddy coat off the ground and followed his instructions, stepping into the warm vehicle.

He got inside and slammed the door. When he pulled the car back on the road, he said, "I've been trying to reach you."

Trapped in a car, she was helpless to escape his masculine power and deep, stirring sexuality. She couldn't look at him without seeing the lips that had made her forget her name, the hands that had caressed her so tenderly. She could almost feel herself once again falling under his spell.

"I need your account information," he continued, "so that I can transfer the stock back to you."

"I don't want it."

"Then I need your account information so that I can pay you for it."

Now she was getting it. He was afraid of a lawsuit, afraid that she would make a big stink at the company and drag down his net worth. Well, he needn't have worried. She had told him once that she was not a hysterical woman and she had meant it. She planned on walking away with whatever dignity she had left.

"Look, Lessa, talk to me. We need to communicate if we're to work together."

"We're not going to be working together, Rick. I'm a minority shareholder. There's no way I'm going to keep my position on the board."

"I'm giving you my support, Lessa. No one can do a damn thing about it."

"You mean, whether they like it or not, I'll stay on as chairman?"

"That's right."

"I don't want to work someplace like this, Rick. How would I justify my position? The president's mistress? Former mistress."

"So take back your stock. You'll be the principal stockholder once again."

"I don't want it back. It was a deal, Rick. Fair and square."

"You can't leave Lawrence Enterprises, Lessa. You said yourself that it's meant to be. It was what your father wanted. And the work you did on the Antigua/Florida deal was very good. You took charge of it and brought it all together without my help. I need someone like that."

"I'm resigning, Rick. It's my Christmas present to the board."

He hesitated. "Lessa, I bought Mara del Ray. It can be yours. To remake, do whatever you want."

So he had bought it after all. "You were smart to buy it. It's a good investment. You'll see."

"Lessa, think about this. You've wanted to be at the helm of Lawrence for years. Don't let your anger toward me get in the way of your dreams."

It was tempting, but she couldn't stay. She couldn't bear the idea of working side by side with Rick, knowing that he didn't care about her. That he never would.

"I thought you weren't a quitter," Rick said.

How dare he insinuate that she was giving up, admitting defeat? It was taking every ounce of courage for her to leave the company she had fought so hard for. "I have no choice. I realize now that although this company still uses my father's name, it's not his anymore. And it hasn't been for a very long time. It's your company, Rick. You worked for it. You deserve it."

"Don't do this, Lessa," he said, pulling in front of the building where the meeting was being held. "You can't walk away from something that you love."

"Thought I loved. But I was wrong." As she looked at him, she felt a stab of sadness. She was no longer talking about the company, but him.

"I'm not going to let you do this," he said, parking the car. "I'm not going to let you walk away like this. What will it take?"

"Why do you care, Rick?"

"Because I…I care about you," he said, taking her hands in his.

The words hung in the air. She wanted to believe him so badly. He slid next to her and pressed his lips against her, gently covering her mouth. She could feel herself letting go, her defenses melting away. She wanted to believe him. And she did. But it wasn't enough.

No matter what they did or how hard they tried, they

could never be partners at Lawrence Enterprises. Despite the fact that she had given it her all and had played the match of a lifetime, she had lost, and one thing she knew was how to accept defeat gracefully. There would be only one victor in this match. She pulled away from Rick and stepped out of the car. As she walked toward the inn, she felt as if her heart were breaking.

I will miss you, Rick Parker, she said in her mind. *I will miss you.*

Fourteen

That night, Rick did something he had not done in a long time. He went home. At least thirty people were crammed into his parent's small house and the result was bedlam. A fire was burning in the fireplace, an oversize tree was stuffed in the corner of the living room, torn pieces of wrapping paper were scattered about and presents were piled all over the place. Most of the children had escaped downstairs, but every now and then the door to the basement would fly open and a child would burst into the room, excitedly talking about Santa Claus. But Rick did not partake in any festivities. He stood off by himself, his mind focused on Lessa. Only hours ago, he had watched Lessa give away the company she loved. Up until the final moment, he had been sure that she would come to her senses and change her mind.

"I'm glad you're home," his sister, Susan, said, walking up to him. "I've forgotten how much fun you are." He knew she was teasing but he was in no mood.

She sighed and motioned for their brother, Russell, to join them. "Rick is in trouble."

"I'm not in trouble," he said. "I just don't like watching someone throw their career away."

"What did you expect?" Susan asked, "That she would go back to work as usual? You just swindled her out of her company. She doesn't want anything to do with you."

"So let her hate me. But giving away the company just hurts herself."

"For one," his sister said, "she hurt more than herself. She hurt you." She sighed deeply. "But I doubt that she realizes that. I'm sure she's convinced you care little for her."

"I tried to talk her out of this."

"I'm sure she felt as if she had little choice. She didn't exactly throw anything away. You took it. And by the time you changed your mind, it was too late. I understand completely why she did what she did. How can she go back to Lawrence Enterprises knowing that she will have to see you every day? It's just too hard."

"What happened after the board meeting?" his brother asked.

"She rode back to the city with one of the assistants." Rick had attempted to talk to her, but she had escaped immediately after her resignation. He had sat there, helpless to stop her as she'd walked out of his life.

"I can't believe you threw away a perfectly good opportunity to improve your serve. I bet she would've given you some lessons," Russell teased, swinging a pretend racket. "Oh well, you're back at the helm of your company, and that's what's important, right?"

"I'm going to resign," Rick announced suddenly. His brother and sister grew quiet and exchanged worried glances. He knew it seemed sudden, but he had never felt so clearheaded in his life. The truth of the matter was that the company he'd fought so long and hard for no longer mattered to him. He had paid too high a price.

"Does Lessa know that?" Russell asked.

"I don't think it would make a damn bit of difference. She doesn't want to be with me."

"She was upset," his sister chimed in. "What did you expect?"

"I told her I cared about her. I don't just toss that out there."

"You *care* about her? What's that supposed to mean? I'll tell you what it doesn't mean. It doesn't mean that you love her."

Rick was silent for a moment. "But I do." He felt like a burden had been lifted from his shoulders. Dammit, he loved her. He *loved* her.

"We know that. But she doesn't."

"Look, I know a thing or two about women," Russell said as Susan rolled her eyes. "And one thing I know is words are not enough. Women need proof. You have to *show* her how you feel."

"She lives with her aunt, right?" asked Susan. "Does she know how you feel?"

He shook his head. "I don't think she's too fond of me."

"Well, that was your first mistake. She loves Lessa

and wants the best for her. Plead your case to the aunt and wrangle an invitation to Christmas dinner."

"Just show up?"

"With an invite."

"Susan's right," Russell said. "If you love her, you're going to have to fight for her. She's not one of your typical women who takes one look at you and swoons and falls into your arms. She's got spunk."

His mother walked over and joined them. "I'm so glad you came for Christmas," she said to Rick.

"I'm afraid he has to leave, Mom," Susan said.

"Business?" she asked.

"No," he said, "not this time."

Susan smiled. As Rick left the room, she said, "Don't be disappointed, Mom. He'll be back next year—and he won't be alone."

"I'm sorry, Gran," Lessa said. "I've lost everything."

"You didn't lose Lawrence Enterprises. Your father did. You did everything you could to get it back."

"Well, I lost the stock."

"You sold it for a fair price." Despite Lessa's protests, Rick had given her the same deal they had promised Sabrina. "I didn't think the loss of some stock is responsible for keeping you up all night." Her aunt took a sip of her tea. "Perhaps you should give him a chance. Let him prove himself. It is Christmas after all."

Lessa looked at her aunt, surprised. She had expected Gran to jump up and down for joy when Lessa had told her she was finished with Rick Parker and Lawrence Enterprises. Instead Gran had looked at her as if she had made the biggest mistake of her life. But what did her aunt expect her to do? Fall into Rick's arms after the way he had treated her? And how could she work with him after what had happened between them?

Her aunt sighed. "This is not the way Christmas is supposed to be spent."

"Oh no, Gran. Please don't give me the spiel about family and kids. I can't take it."

"Actually, I was talking about the lack of eggnog."

"I told you, Chapman's was out."

"Oh, Lessa, I just feel so bad for you. Stuck here with an old woman and no eggnog."

"I guarantee you there's no place I'd rather be." That was true, wasn't it? She wouldn't want to be wrapped in Rick's arms. No, sir. Lessa finished off her tea. "It's wonderful that there's snow," she said, eager to change the subject. The rain had turned to snow shortly after dusk. "When's the last time it snowed in New York on Christmas?"

"A white Christmas," her aunt said. "How romantic. Maybe you should invite Rick over."

"Invite him over?" Had her aunt heard a word of what she had said? "Rick is probably off in some exotic locale drinking a piña colada and dancing with a beautiful woman. I'm sure he's forgotten all about me by now."

"I'm not so certain. From what you've told me, I think he was as surprised as you by the whole turn of events."

Lessa closed her eyes as the wave of pain washed over her. She wanted to believe that; she really did. She would like nothing better than to think that Rick was by himself, mourning her loss. But she knew better. And she could not allow herself to feel sad. It did no good. She had made her decision.

"It doesn't have to be like this, Lessa."

"There's no choice, Gran. When people love each other, they treat each other decently. You don't have deceit and lies. Real love doesn't hurt like this."

"You've been reading too many storybooks. Real life doesn't always work that way. I never told you about your uncle and me. We dated for two years, and I was madly in love. I thought we were going to get married. And then he went off to the war."

"And then he came home and married you."

"That's the story we've always told. I didn't mention what really happened because it bothered him too much."

"What are you talking about? He loved you. He thought about you every day he was away."

"When he came home, I found out that he was engaged to someone else."

Lessa couldn't believe what she was hearing. Her uncle? The kindly bespectacled man who had worshipped her aunt?

"Apparently he never got any of my letters, but I didn't know that then. He assumed I didn't care about him, and naturally, when I found out about his engagement, I assumed the same thing about him. It broke my heart. Well, he went off and married that other woman. And you know what? It was the best thing that ever happened to me."

"Uncle Stan was married before? Did Dad know this?"

"Of course. But what difference did it make? The point of the story is that he eventually came back. And you know what? I had changed—for the better. I was so much stronger than I had been. I knew I could make it on my own. And he knew what he wanted all along.

Me. If he hadn't married that other woman, he might've always wondered if he made the right decision. Instead, I was appreciated. Very appreciated. Until the day he died, he would've done anything to make me happy."

"So what are you saying? Do you think Rick will go off and marry someone else? Or do you think I will?"

"I think that Rick learned a valuable lesson here. And I believe him when he said he cared about you." She smiled. "I think I know a thing or two about men."

"I can't think about Rick, Gran. I have to move on with my life. I'm going to look for a little property to buy. I'm going start over, build my own company from scratch. And I'm thinking about going back to tennis. Not as a player, but a teacher. I could combine my knowledge of resorts with my love for tennis. Maybe I could start a camp somewhere."

There was a knock on the door.

"Why, who in the world could that be?" her aunt said, feigning surprise.

"Maybe it's Santa," Lessa said, glancing at her aunt suspiciously. What was she up to?

Lessa got up and opened the door—to Rick Parker. He stood before her, covered in snow.

"Rick," her aunt said, brushing past Lessa to get to him.

"Wh-What are you doing here?" Lessa asked, so surprised she could barely speak.

"Your aunt said she needed eggnog."

"Oh, you found some." Gran said. "You're a dear, Rick. Thank you."

"This isn't funny." Lessa gave her aunt the evil eye.

"Who's joking?" Rick asked. "I had to go to three different stores to find this."

"Come in," her aunt said warmly, taking his coat and the container of eggnog. "I think this'll need some brandy, don't you?" She stopped and turned back toward the doorway. "Would you look at that," she said, motioning above Rick and Lessa where a small piece of greenery had been tied to the light fixture. "Mistletoe." She looked at Lessa and winked.

When she was gone, Rick stared into Lessa's eyes. "I told you once, Lessa. I don't give up."

"Look, Rick, I don't want to be a part of Lawrence Enterprises anymore."

"I'm not asking you to." He reached inside his jacket. "I just stopped by to give you something." He pulled out a manila envelope. "Open it," he said, handing it to her.

She ripped open the envelope. It was the deed to Mara del Ray. "I don't understand…."

"I'm giving it to you. A chance to build your own hotel."

He came over on Christmas Eve to sell her a property? "How much do you want for it?"

"I don't want money," he said, looking at her hungrily.

"What do you want?"

"A partnership."

"What about Lawrence Enterprises?"

"I'm resigning. I want to build a corporation step by step, just like your parents did. I was thinking that a tennis camp might be a good place to start." He put his hands on her waist. "You spoke once about expectations…well, I didn't expect this either. I can't seem to stay away from you. I don't *want* to stay away from you."

They were words she had waited a lifetime to hear,

but it was the heartrending tenderness of his gaze that melted her remaining defenses.

"I know what it's like to be frightened of love, Lessa," he said. "I know what it's like to close off your heart. I've spent years like that. But I also know that true love is damned hard to find. It took me a long time to find you, Lessa. And now that I have, I'm not about to lose you."

As she looked into his eyes, she was filled with the same sense of desire that had haunted her from the first moment she'd seen him. She moved toward him slowly, and then, standing underneath the mistletoe, she tentatively pressed her lips to his.

He kissed her back, gently and tenderly, a lover's kiss. She wrapped her arms around his neck and pulled him toward her, knotting her fingers through his thick, wavy hair. "Thank you for my Christmas present," she said.

"That wasn't your Christmas present." He reached inside his coat pocket and pulled out a small box. "*This* is your Christmas present."

Her heart jumped into her throat as she took it and opened it. Inside, nestled on satin, was an emerald-cut diamond ring.

"I love you, Lessa, and I want to be with you. You make the world a better place."

She was too excited to speak. She just stood there, staring at the ring, not believing her ears.

"Say you'll marry me, Lessa," he whispered. "Give me a reason to like Christmas again."

"Yes, Rick, I'll marry you." She threw her arms around his neck and kissed him with all her might. When she was finished, she said the three words she had wanted to say for a long, long time. "I love you."

* * *

The wedding was held exactly three months later, on the grounds of their first joint venture, a Florida resort that specialized in tennis. It was intended to be a low-key affair, with only close friends and relatives. For Rick, Lessa discovered, that meant two hundred people, who filled Mara del Ray to capacity. And Lessa loved every moment of it. The entire Parker clan had accepted her and her aunt as welcome additions.

Lessa and Rick were married on a clear, sunny day in the hotel garden. Lessa wore a sleeveless white chiffon gown and walked down a stone path toward the most handsome man she had ever seen.

As Rick watched her walk toward him, he had no doubt that Lessa was the woman he had been waiting for all those years. With her by his side, he knew that anything was possible. She, and she alone, was the treasure for which he had combed the world.

Afterward they celebrated on the beach, complete with blazing tiki lights and a steel drum band. The guests feasted on fresh fish that had been caught that day. It was a fitting celebration for a former pirate. Rick took her hand and kissed it, giving her a smile that made her tingle all the way to her toes.

She and Rick stood at the water's edge, discussing their honeymoon plans with Susan, Rick's sister. "What made you decide on the Bahamas?" Susan asked. "After all, you've been to so many romantic places. I thought you'd pick something really exotic."

"Betty suggested it," Lessa said, nodding toward Rick's secretary. Instead of retiring, Betty and her husband had moved to Florida a little bit early and Betty now worked for them part-time. In fact, they had received many inquiries from former employees of Lawrence, asking if they might join the new venture.

"There's a property there we're interested in," Lessa added with a smile. In fact, they were considering buying Sabrina's resort. Sabrina, in fact, was the one'd who suggested it to them. She had decided that being the owner of a large corporation was adversely affecting her love life, and so she had decided to sell her business and embark on a trip around the world with her sailing instructor.

"Rick!" his sister said, swatting him. "It's your honeymoon!"

"It was my idea," Lessa said. "It seemed to make sense." The transition from enemy to beloved had gone as seamlessly as the beginning of their new corporation. Rick and Lessa were both equal shareholders and partners. And although Rick was still the same tough negotiator he had been at Lawrence, as a lover and husband he was unrivaled. There were few grievances. They had melded together in the boardroom as easily as the bedroom. In fact, she was having the time of her life. For once, she had no doubt that she was in the right field, no doubt that this was what she was meant to do.

"Well, that doesn't sound very romantic to me. A working honeymoon."

But Lessa knew different. They were simply taking a tour. There would be plenty of time for…other activities.

"Mom," Susan's youngest son said, tugging on her dress. "Richard's swimming in the pool," he said, referring to his seven-year-old brother.

"It's okay," Lessa said. "There's a lifeguard."

"But he went swimming with his clothes on."

As Susan ran off to attend to her son, Lessa saw her aunt sitting under a palm tree. She was fanning herself as she sipped some frothy pink drink with an umbrella.

"I'll be right back," Lessa said to Rick.

"What are you thinking about?" she asked her aunt as she sat beside her on the sand.

"I'm just thinking about that mistletoe. See? Aren't you glad you didn't throw it out or stick it in the closet?"

"You think this is all due to mistletoe?"

"Well, I certainly got my wish," Gran said. "And so did you."

Lessa caught the eyes of the man she loved, and smiled. "And then some. I can't wait to see what you ask for next year."

Her aunt nodded toward the beach at the children playing. "It might be nice to have some children around."

Lessa just laughed. As it turned out, she had been thinking the exact same thing.

After the wedding, she and Rick retired to the private bungalow they had built for their home. The French doors were open and a warm breeze blew the silk sheers. Lessa stepped outside, followed by Rick.

"Gran asked me to give you this," he said, holding out a small brown paper bag.

Lessa opened the bag and peeked inside. She laughed as she pulled out a sprig of mistletoe. She held it up to the moonlight and said, "My aunt swears that mistletoe is associated with miracles. You simply hold it and make a wish."

"Should we test it out?" he asked.

She put a hand on her belly. "I should warn you that

I have a feeling I know what she's wishing for next Christmas."

"Next Christmas?" he asked, flashing her a devilish smile. "Let's see, April, May, June…" He counted out the remaining months. "Nine months exactly. We better start working on this miracle right away."

And holding the mistletoe over their heads, he gave her a long, passionate kiss.

* * * * *

Tycoon Takes Revenge

by Anna DePalo

**Infamous playboy Noah Whittaker
gives gossip columnist Kayla Jones
a taste of her own medicine, but will
they find that love is far sweeter
than revenge?**

On sale
December 2005

Only from Silhouette Books.

COMING NEXT MONTH

#1693 NAME YOUR PRICE—Barbara McCauley
Dynasties: The Ashtons
His family's money and power tore them apart, but will time be
able to heal the wounds of this priceless love?

#1694 TRUST ME—Caroline Cross
Men of Steele
An ex-navy SEAL is in over his head when he has to rescue the
woman who broke his heart years ago.

#1695 A MOST SHOCKING REVELATION—Kristi Gold
Texas Cattleman's Club: The Secret Diary
A sexy sheriff is torn between his duty and his desire for a
woman looking for her own brand of justice.

#1696 A BRIDE BY CHRISTMAS—Joan Elliott Pickart
Is this wedding planner really cursed never to find true love—
or has Mr. Right just not appeared...until now?

#1697 TYCOON TAKES REVENGE—Anna DePalo
An infamous playboy gives a gossip columnist a taste of her own
medicine, but finds that love is far sweeter than revenge.

#1698 TROPHY WIVES—Jan Colley
What will this wounded millionaire find beneath this rich girl's
carefree facade?

SDCNM1105